THE WAVES
KEEP CRASHING

THE WAVES KEEP CRASHING

ELLIE KEEHN

proving
press

Book Design & Production:
Columbus Publishing Lab
www.ColumbusPublishingLab.com

Copyright © 2020 by Ellie Keehn

LCCN: 2020918819

Paperback ISBN: 978-1-63337-441-6
E-Book ISBN: 978-1-63337-442-3

Printed in the United States of America
1 3 5 7 9 10 8 6 4 2

CHAPTER 1

ACTION!

I began to panic as the boat drew closer and closer to the trees. I tried to steer it away, but it was too late. I was prepared to crash when suddenly…

"Cut!"

Thud. My kayak made contact with the wall of the mangroves yet again.

"Miss Ganson!" Mr. Davis yelled. Then, he lowered his voice, trying to stay calm. "*Please* try not to crash."

"I'm so sorry," I said, as my face turned red. "I'll get it this time."

I was in the midst of shooting a commercial that promoted tourism at Captiva Island, our small town in southern Florida. I'd signed up to simply be filmed kayaking through a trail, but I kept crashing. I was normally very good at it, but when I arrived at the set, Mr. Davis intimidated me. He was a perfectionist with a grumpy persona. Anyone could sense that he wished he was directing movies, instead of local commercials.

"Alright. All you have to do is kayak a few feet and pretend this is the best thing you've ever done. Got it? It shouldn't be this hard. Okay? Let's try again. Action!"

I started to row with a smile on my face. But out of the corner of my eye, I could see him staring at me intensely. Before I knew it, I had veered to the left and crashed into the trees again.

"Oh, for crying out loud!" he yelled, as he threw his hands up. Then, when he leaned over to lecture me some more, his boat tipped and he fell into the bay.

About thirty minutes later, after he recovered and I finally perfected the shot, we were done. I rowed back to the dock in total embarrassment. I could almost feel Mr. Davis's resentful laser eyes on my back.

Then I noticed a figure jumping up and down on the dock. To my surprise, my best friend, Penelope Miller, was standing there clapping for me. She had dark brown, perfect skin. Her eyes were brown and cheerful, but most of the time they had a competitive edge. During high school, she was the captain of the volleyball team, played basketball, and held records for the high school girls' 100 meters, 200 meters and 100 meter hurdles. Like always, her curly brown hair was tied in a bun. She was wearing a volleyball t-shirt, Nike shorts, and flip-flops.

"Nelly! What are you doing here?" I asked, as I held out my hand for help.

"I had to see my best friend, the famous actress, of course!" she teased, as she leaned over in a royal bow.

"Shut up," I laughed. "Why are you here?"

Then my other best friend, Elizabeth Rhymes, ran up to me, grabbed my arms, and looked me straight in the eyes.

"Emmi! You *need* to get dressed! Your show got pushed up an hour and you weren't replying to your boss. Your mom sent us over to rush you there. Go, go, go!"

Liz had tan skin and bright green eyes that were looking at me fiercely. She had dark brown hair that was curled and down to her shoulders. She was wearing jean shorts and a sleeveless top. Like always, she was carrying her hot pink purse that she brought to all of our activities. Somehow, whenever we needed something, it was always in that bag. She was our most faithful and devoted fan. Nelly and I made fun of her for it, but honestly, without her we would fall apart.

The three of us have been best friends ever since we were all six years old. We all lived close to each other and took the same classes throughout high school. Our families were so close that we were basically sisters.

When we were little, we thought our names were too long to say when we talked to each other. Dad would snicker and joke, "I know, right! It takes a *whole extra second!*" Because we were so young, we had no clue that he was teasing us. As a result, we made up nicknames. Ever since, we've been called Nelly, Liz, and Emmi.

"Okay, I'll hurry," I replied. The show that got pushed up an hour was a 'mermaid' show in my town's local aquarium. I had to dress up like one and swim around, while little kids gawked at me.

"I'm serious! Your show starts in one hour and you have so much to do. I'll go thank Mr. Davis for giving you this oppor-"

"No, no, no," I said with alarm. "Let's just go."

"Emmi, don't be rude. I'll be right back."

I rolled my eyes but let her go. She walked towards Mr. Davis, while Nelly and I went to the car.

As long as I could remember, I had been swimming. Living in Florida, who wouldn't be? But for me, it was different. Swimming meant everything. I was on the varsity girls' swim team all throughout high school, and I was the captain starting my sophomore year. Every job I'd ever had involved swimming. In addition to all of this, I was acknowledged for my ability to hold my breath for an extraordinary amount of time. Swimming also opened up new relationships and strengthened old ones. It had made me a better, more successful person. Everything I'd ever done had been in the water. Swimming made me feel more alive than anything else in the world.

I couldn't imagine life without it.

CHAPTER 2

I'M PRETTY TIRED

"**C**an you drive the car a little faster? You're not going to have much time! You have to do makeup, do your-"

Then Nelly rolled down Liz's window, so that we couldn't hear the rest of her sentence. After a few seconds of trying to yell over the blasting wind, Liz gave up. She sat back, crossed her arms, and glared. Finally, Nelly rolled the window back up.

"Oh, I'm sorry," Nelly began, as she pretended to be clueless. "Were you saying something?"

"Yes. I just want to make sure-"

Again, she rolled down the window.

"Gah!" Liz screamed.

The two of them had been at each other's throats for as long as they'd been friends. They were like sisters that constantly fought over every little thing. They thoroughly enjoyed making each other mad. But also like sisters, they loved each other. None of their arguments actually damaged their relationship. Most of the time, they just annoyed me.

When we arrived, Nelly rolled up the window and turned off the car.

"Was that *really* necessary?" Liz huffed.

"Yes. You were criticizing my driving and repeating yourself. It was making me crazy."

"So was the wind!"

"It was better than your voice."

"Stop!" I interrupted. "I'm already late. Liz and I will go to the dressing room and Nelly, you can go find seats."

Liz and I got to the changing room to find my makeup artist, Kelly, pacing.

"Finally!" she exclaimed.

"I know. I'm sorry. I had the commercial today and with the show being moved up-"

"No time for explaining. Just put on the tail, while I do your makeup."

"I'll do her hair!" Liz said excitedly. She loved doing hair, specifically mine. She's always called it fluffy or something.

When it was time for the show to start, I did my breathing routine and I dropped into the tank. I couldn't say I liked this job. The only reason I took it was because I needed some extra money for college in the fall. But I had to admit, I fit the role perfectly. I had tan skin, naturally dirty blonde hair, and dark blue eyes that looked like the ocean. Also, I could hold my breath for an abnormally long amount of time, so I didn't have to go up for air often.

When I saw Liz and Nelly surrounded by about 30 bright-eyed kids, I almost started laughing right there.

"Wow, it's a real mermaid!" a little girl in the front row squealed.

"I can't believe it!" said a boy somewhere in the middle.

"She's gorgeous!" said a voice I recognized. I followed it, and there was Elliot Peters, my boyfriend, sitting with his little brother, Eddy. Elliot was about 6 feet tall with tan skin and dark brown hair. I loved his puppy-dog brown eyes that were accented by his black-framed glasses. He looked so relaxed in his blue t-shirt with gray shorts and sandals. My hand went straight to my neck where my silver heart necklace was. I laced it through my fingers and smiled. Then I waved at him and continued my performance.

When I left the aquarium, my biggest fans were waiting for me.

"Great job, Emmi!" Elliot smiled, as he grabbed my hand.

"Thanks."

"I almost started to believe you were real!" Liz added with praise.

Eddy gave me a high-five, as we continued to talk.

"Hey, Emmi, I was wondering if you want to hang out tonight?" Elliot asked.

I scrunched my nose and said, "Um, ya know, I've had a really long day. I'm pretty tired."

He opened his mouth right away, then closed it. He scratched his head and said, "Oh. Okay... I, I guess I'll text you later then."

I squeezed his hand and kissed him. Then he took Eddy's hand and they walked away. When they left, I noticed that both Liz and Nelly were frowning at me.

"What?"

"How long has it been since you guys have spent any time together?" Liz questioned.

"Just now," I said, as I pointed down.

"You spoke like five sentences to each other," Nelly said with wide eyes.

"We know things have been hectic because of school ending, but *I've* seen Elliot more than you have," Liz said in an accusing tone.

"Yes, we haven't been hanging out as much as we used to."

"It's been a few months, Emmi."

"I know, I know! Guys, Elliot and I have been together for three years. We'll be okay. Now can we just drop this? I really am tired."

They hesitated, but followed me to the car.

When I got home, I kicked my bright orange flip-flops onto the shoe mat and walked into the kitchen. My family was doing dishes in an assembly line, like always. We did everything as a family, even chores. Mom looked up and smiled.

"Hi dear. How was your day?" Even though we looked a lot alike with our dirty blonde hair and tan skin, Mom had green eyes, unlike my blue ones. She was also on her swim team during high school, but I had better times.

"Are you hungry? We just finished, and we made your fav-" Dad started.

"Emmi!" my brother, Liam, yelled. He put his plate down and ran over to give me a hug.

He was eight years old and was, obviously, a lot shorter than me. He had brown scraggly hair that he always 'forgot' to brush. He had blue eyes and glasses that had green and black frames with a little Ninja turtle on the side. He was wearing a red t-shirt that had a picture of a shark on it and black shorts. Liam looked *exactly* like Dad.

"Hi Liam," I said, hugging him back.

"As I was saying," Dad said, "are you hungry? We made your favorite."

"Yes, it smells amazing. I'll be right back."

When I got to my bedroom, I sat on the bed and took out my phone. It was only eight o'clock. I was beginning to feel really bad about not being with Elliot, so I decided to text him.

Emmi: ur coming 2 my swim meet tmrw right?

Elliot: Wouldn't miss it :)

CHAPTER 3

YOUR BREAKFAST IS SERVED

The next morning I was awakened by the most relentless, horrible, heart-wrenching and ear-piercing noise known to every teenager: the beeping of an alarm clock. I tried to ignore it, but it kept going. I pulled my arm out from underneath the covers and turned it off a little too rough. It slipped off my side table and landed on the floor with a thud. I thought about leaving it there, but then I remembered that today was my first club swim meet.

At the end of my senior year, I was devastated to be done with competitive swimming. To give my favorite sport one last hurrah, I joined a club team. We were amazing. We had so many of the fastest swimmers from the regular season that there was no doubt we'd do great.

"Good morning! We made breakfast for you, so get dressed fast!" Mom said, as she burst in without knocking. I stayed in bed with my face pressed into the pillow and wished for just a few more minutes of sleep. But Mom pulled off the covers and forced me to get up.

When she left, I sat up and brushed the tangled hair out of my face. I squinted around the room in search of my glasses. (I wore contacts during the day.) When I put them on, the cold plastic made my warm, still half-asleep body shiver.

The bag that held my swimsuit, swim cap, goggles, and anything else that I needed for the meet was lying on the floor. Next to it was a t-shirt, black sweatpants, my tennis shoes, and a blue sweatshirt that had a picture of our mascot, an animated bull shark. In big gray letters it read: BULL SHARKS BITE! The back had a list of all my teammates' names on it.

I looked at the alarm clock and grunted. I'd been sitting in bed for five minutes. As I pushed myself up, my muscles felt like they hadn't moved in a century. I must've slept well.

I walked downstairs and was greeted by the stench of burning food. I knew instantly that Dad was making pancakes.

"Honey, will you grab the spatula?" he asked, as he struggled to keep more pancakes from burning. He was holding the bowl of batter, most of it dripping down the side and onto his arm, while the other hand tried to grab plates from the cabinet. My brother was trying to flip the pancakes using a potato peeler. *Seriously?* Mom was hastily searching all the drawers to find a spatula. She eventually gave up and moved the burnt, oddly-shaped pancakes onto a plate with her hands. All of this was happening with a cloud of smoke hanging over their heads.

When the haze finally cleared, I sat down at the island.

"Your breakfast is served," Dad said goofily, as he set a plate down in front of me. The pancake was charcoal black and smelled like smoke. It was in a distorted shape that looked like a giraffe but also a squiggly fish.

"Umm… Dad? Is this supposed to be something?"

"Well, yes," he said as his smile faltered. "Can't you tell? It's a medal."

"Yeah, because you guys are going to win today!" Liam added.

"I get it, Liam," I said with a forced smile. Then I looked at my plate and tried not to reveal my revulsion. It was cute that they did this for me, but it didn't look edible.

"On second thought, I'm not that hungry. I'll just meet you guys at the pool." I tried to ignore everyone's disappointed expressions.

"Okay," Mom said, trying not to sound annoyed after all the work Dad and Liam did. "We'll see you there."

"Good luck!" my dad and brother chimed in unison.

When they weren't looking, I snagged a protein bar from the pantry.

CHAPTER 4

BULL SHARKS BITE

"Alright, girls, we can do this. Swim your race, encourage your teammates, and do your best." Our coach was very confident in us and didn't need to get too carried away with the pep talks. After that, we all put our hands in the middle.

"1, 2, 3, Bull Sharks!" we all cheered.

I wasn't scheduled to swim until the second to the last race, so I had plenty of time to go find my friends. I left the locker room and started searching the stands. My eyes landed on Liz. She had a temporary tattoo of a shark on her cheek and she was holding a sign that read 'Go Bull Sharks!' Sitting next to her was Nelly, who couldn't have cared less about the small paper tattoo that Liz was trying to force into her hand. I walked up the steps towards them and saw Liz's hot pink bag sitting next to her. I reached into it and found my bright orange water bottle with four ice cubes in the top.

"Thanks, Liz, I totally forgot a water." They stopped arguing and both turned to look at me.

"Hi Emmi!" Nelly exclaimed, while she moved over to give me a hug. "Do you care if I don't wear this ridiculous tattoo?"

"I guess not. At least I have one good friend," I teased. Nelly rolled her eyes and slapped the temporary tattoo out of Liz's hand.

"Hey!" Liz said, as she reached down to pick up the paper. "I'm just being supportive! Nelly, you're not even wearing Bull Shark colors."

As they continued to jab at each other, I searched the rest of the stands for my family. I saw them just as Liam saw me and waved. I smiled and waved back, while continuing to scour the audience. Someone was missing.

"Have you guys seen Elliot? I thought he'd be here by now."

"Haven't seen him. I'm sure he'll show though," Nelly replied.

"Don't worry about him!" Liz huffed. "Get down there with your team. We'll cheer you on." I hugged them again, went back down the steps and jogged over to where my team was sitting.

The first person to swim was a girl who was a year younger than me. She won her race, but it was close. Although we were winning, the scores were a little tighter than we originally thought they would be.

Then it was my turn.

I stepped up to the diving board and shook out my arms and legs. I looked to my left and saw one of the swimmers from the Fighting Seals, the second place team. I recognized her from one of our regular season meets. I couldn't remember which school she was from, but I knew she was fast.

I faced the long strip of pool in front of me and did what I always do. I blocked out all the noise around me and imagined the crashing of waves, the bloop-blooping of bubbles rising to the surface, and the rush of kicking feet underwater. I took deep breaths in my nose and out my mouth, as I pulled the goggles over my eyes. The referee put the whistle to his lips and every swimmer bent down in unison. Then the whistle blew.

I dove into the pool and swam with all my strength. The water churned around me as I fought against it. Momentum pushed me to the opposite wall and as I made the turn, my ears broke the surface and I heard the crowd cheering crazily. I was ahead. My adrenaline kicked in and pulled me all the way to the finish.

I won my race by a mile! As it turned out, the girl from the Fighting Seals had a late start and got fourth place. At that point, we knew we had secured the win. And by the sound of it, so did everyone in the stands.

The whole team was talking in the locker room when one girl stood up on a bench. "Hey girls! I'm having a party at my house tonight to celebrate our win. Invite anyone you want," she announced. Everyone cheered and started talking about the party. I was going to bring Nelly and Liz, of course. After that, we left the locker room, as the winners were being announced.

"Third place, the Blue Whales!"

"Second place, the Fighting Seals!"

"And finally, your champions, the Bull Sharks!"

As the crowd and everyone on my team celebrated, I looked in the stands and saw my friends and family.

But still no Elliot.

CHAPTER 5

I TOLD YOU SO

"I'm so happy for you guys!" Nelly gushed. "It was so fun watching everyone swim."

After my meet, the three of us had gone back to Liz's house to get ready for the party. We were relaxing in her room when she came out of her huge walk-in closet holding two dresses.

"Which one? Navy or dark blue?"

"They're the same color," Nelly replied.

"What are you talking about? There is a very defined contrast," Liz declared. "And you're not wearing that, Nelly. You can wear whichever dress I don't."

"What I'm wearing is fine. Besides, I don't want to match you."

"They're not the same color!" Liz yelled, as she rolled her eyes and trudged back into her closet.

Suddenly, my phone buzzed.

Elliot: Can I call u?

"It's Elliot," I said, as I turned my phone around to show Nelly.

Obviously, he never showed up to my meet. If he would've texted to tell me he couldn't come, I would've been less upset. But I had been telling him the whole week how nervous I was for this. Every time we talked, he said he couldn't wait to watch me. I couldn't believe he would just skip something that was so important to me.

"What are you going to say?" Liz asked, peeking her head out of the closet.

"I guess I'll just tell him that I'm disappointed."

"Emmi…" Nelly started.

"What?"

"Just… don't get too mad. Remember what we were talking about yesterday? This is the first time he's missed anything of yours, but you've definitely missed events of his."

"Nelly, this meet was so important to me. I've told him how I love seeing him in the crowd and cheering me on; it makes me less nervous. He also told me that he wouldn't miss this meet, and he did. I'm sorry I wanted my boyfriend to come," I snapped. Then I got up and walked to the bathroom without another word.

I closed the door behind me, as I started to scroll through my contacts. I clicked the call button and he picked up right away.

"Hey," he said.

"Hi…"

"Em-"

"Today was a really big day for me. I was counting on seeing you in the crowd. You're lucky I didn't know you weren't there until after my race. I've told you how nervous I get," I said harshly. "This was my last first meet ever, and you missed it. It was important to me that you would be there. I'm just really disappointed."

There was a long pause on his end.

"Geesh, Emmi," he said with disgust. "When Eddy and I were doing some work on the front porch before the meet, he dropped a hammer on his toe. I was worried it might've been broken, so I took him to the hospital right away. I didn't go inside to grab my phone, so I couldn't text you. And to be honest, I wasn't really thinking about hurting your feelings, while my brother was getting an x-ray. Anyway, we just got home, so I thought I'd let you know why I wasn't there."

I was at a loss for words. My face felt hot.

"Uh," I stammered.

"I'm sorry I didn't make it, but should it have been that big a deal anyway?" he questioned. In an accusing tone, he said, "You know what? You miss my events, bail on me, ignore me all the time, and I never complain. I can't make it to one stupid meet and this is how you react?"

"Elliot, I'm sorry. I didn't-"

"Whatever," he interrupted.

"Can we at least talk at this party my teammate is having tonight?" My vision blurred with tears. He and I rarely fought and when we did, he never interrupted apologies.

"Actually, I can't make it. I won't be making it to anything from now on. I think we need a little space, Emmi. But that's okay because you don't really have time for a boyfriend anyway."

The phone beeped, as he hung up and tears spilled from my eyes. I looked in the mirror and tried to comprehend what had just happened. I knew we hadn't been seeing each other as much. I also knew that he was always so supportive of me, and I wasn't always there when he wanted me to be. But I didn't realize that it had bothered him so much. I wiped my eyes, shoved open the door and stormed into Liz's room.

"How'd it go?" she asked.

"I… I think we broke up," I answered.

They both looked at me with the same expression, and it wasn't shock. It was pity.

"Why are you looking at me like that?"

"Emmi, we told you-" Nelly started.

"Hold on," I interrupted. "My boyfriend of three years just dumped me and the first thing you're going to say is *I told you so?*"

"Well, we didn't think he'd *break up* with you, but we knew something was going to have to change," Liz said cautiously.

"Wow," I said, as I started to gather my things. "Thanks for the comfort. My best friends in the whole world, ladies and gentlemen!"

"Come on…"

"Nope. I'm leaving. See ya later," I said, as I threw open the door, stormed down the stairs, and headed to my car.

"Wait!" Nelly said, running after me into the driveway. I stopped and turned around. She looked at me with fire in her eyes.

"What?" I yelled.

"Stop taking this out on us. This isn't our fault! All we did was warn you about something you didn't want to hear. I'm not the one in the relationship and even I can clearly see that you are not putting in any time or effort. You've been dating for three years and you've gotten comfortable. That's okay. But being comfortable with a relationship doesn't mean putting it behind everything else. To put it plainly, you're taking advantage of a really good guy. You're shutting him out and he doesn't deserve that."

It felt like she had stabbed me right in the heart. Deep down, I knew she was right. But I just *had* to be stubborn.

"Well, he's single now. So if you think he's *such a great person* why don't you just go date him!"

"What the-"

"Go beat me at being a girlfriend. I'm sure you will. You always have to win at everything. Look at yourself right now! Instead of trying to make me feel better, you're proving your point at the cost of my feelings. Oh well. It's okay. You won, Nelly!" I screamed.

I wanted her to yell back. I wanted her to crush my enormous ego and help me be a better person. But instead, she stood up straight, wrinkled her brow, narrowed her eyes at me and walked back inside.

As soon as I started driving, my phone dinged with some texts from our swim team group chat. I realized that I was definitely *not* in the mood to party. When I parked in my driveway, I lied and texted that my family was throwing a surprise party for me and I couldn't make it.

I walked into the house and slammed the door behind me.

"Emmi? I thought the party started at six?" Mom asked when she heard me.

"I'm not going," I replied dryly.

"Uh oh, should I take off the pool cover?" Dad asked. Every time I was not in a good mood, I would go to the pool to think or calm down before I could talk. My family knew my routine.

"Yes, please."

I went to my room to change into a swimsuit, then dove right into the pool and let myself sink to the bottom of the deep end.

I stayed down there for a while and thought about what had just happened. I had never felt worse, knowing that my three best friends probably hated me. We had never been in a fight that bad.

I watched the bubbles rise around me as my mood sank. One good thing about being underwater was that no one could see me cry. I felt, for once, so lonely.

I felt like I was drowning, but in something worse than water.

CHAPTER 6

A LONG RIDE

"**M**om, I'm not feeling well," I coughed. "I really don't think I can go."

"Emmi, you've never missed a brunch with the Millers and the Rhymes. You even insisted on going when you had the chicken pox in fifth grade."

It was true. Each January, our families bought passes from Captiva Dolphin Cruises for the year. Almost every Sunday since the fourth grade, all of us had gone on the dolphin watches to eat brunch and catch up. It was normally what I looked forward to every week, but this Sunday was different. I still didn't want to talk about the fight the three of us had. I definitely couldn't face them again today.

"Besides, I think we're having French toast. No one can resist that." When I didn't respond, she dropped her smile. "I'm not taking no for an answer. You are getting on that boat, whether you feel sick or not."

I held my stomach as if it felt bad and cried, "Mom! I'm going to puke!"

"Hon, are you sure this doesn't have anything to do with the fact that you came home upset last night?" She was definitely not buying my sick act.

"No, Mom, I'm not upset." I pushed my covers off and got out of bed as I said, "I'll be down soon." She stepped out of my room and came back in holding a flowing blue sundress.

"I bought this for you when I went shopping yesterday. Do you want to wear it?"

"Sure," I mumbled.

When I was done getting dressed, I walked downstairs to find Dad and Liam sitting at the island. They were dressed up in khaki shorts and polos. Dad was wearing the black pair of sunglasses that he always wore, while Liam was wearing cheap ones to look like Dad.

"We're ready to go," Mom said, as she grabbed her purse from the table. She was wearing a long white sundress with brown sandals. I was wearing the dress she bought me with espadrille sandals. Along with a shell bracelet, I was still wearing the silver heart necklace.

As we walked out, it sank in that I had to see Nelly and Liz. I pouted and closed the door behind me. All I wanted was for something to happen so that I wouldn't be forced to have a conversation with them.

When we arrived, Nelly's mom, Laney, hollered, "Bethany! Tom!" as she smiled and gave my parents a hug. She was standing next to her husband, John, who always talked about superheroes with Liam. Nelly's older brother, Tommy, who was home from college for the summer and her younger brother, Jack, a sophomore in high school, grinned when Liam ran over and gave them fist bumps. Since we were the last ones there, Laney asked, "What took you guys so long?"

"Someone didn't want to get out of bed this morning," Dad said, while looking at me. I frowned.

"Hi Emmi! Hello Liam!" Liz's mom, Catherine, chimed in as she gave Liam and me a hug. She was with her husband, Ben, and Liz's ten-year-old twin sisters, Madison and Melissa.

"Hi Mrs. Rhymes," I said unenthusiastically.

"Can we just go?" I heard Nelly say. I looked towards her. She and Liz were standing shoulder to shoulder by the entrance to the boat. In addition to their uncomfortable expressions, I noticed that they were wearing the same sundress. And...

"Mom!" I whispered in anger.

"Yes?"

"You got the three of us matching dresses?"

"Yes! Isn't it a cute surprise?"

I rolled my eyes and looked away. I was so embarrassed. If the three of us weren't in a fight, we would've thought this was hilarious. The problem was, we *were* in a fight and it wasn't funny. I groaned and we walked to the boat.

This was going to be a long ride.

CHAPTER 7

UH, MORE COFFEE ANYONE?

As soon as we were all aboard, we were thrown into what seemed like never-ending awkwardness. All of our parents wouldn't stop taking pictures of us in our *stupid* matching sundresses. We all fake smiled and were silently thankful we had already had our graduation parties. We wouldn't have wanted to be reminded of this painful moment when we saw these pictures on display.

After at least thirty minutes of pictures and people saying that we were "so cute," we sat at a table below deck for brunch. I was across from Nelly and Liz.

"Hey," Liz said, while looking down at her empty water glass. Neither of us answered.

Finally, the waiters brought out French toast, bacon and coffee. We started to eat, while our parents hammered us with questions that included how our summers were going, how college was for Tommy, how dance was for the twins, and so on. We all answered politely, until the topic of my swim meet came up.

"So," Liz's dad asked, "how did your meet go yesterday, Emmi?" I barely looked up.

"It went fine," I said with no more detail.

Nelly's mom added, "I heard you girls won. How'd you do individually?" I remembered that was the same question Elliot asked before we broke up.

"Fine," I said rudely. The table went silent.

"Uh, well, how was the party you invited the girls to? I know they said it was fun," Liz's mom commented. I stopped trying to get more French toast on my fork and looked up.

"You went to the party?" I asked Nelly and Liz loudly. They looked at each other but didn't answer. The whole table was launched into silence. All that could be heard were the rolling waves and the clanking of forks against plates.

"Uh, more coffee anyone?" Dad asked.

"I can't believe this," I muttered. I pushed back my chair, threw my napkin down, stood up, and stormed away from the table.

I trudged up to the dolphin look-out point. No one was there because everyone on the boat was still eating. I sat on the rail and looked out at the water. There were dolphins happily jumping in and out of the waves. I wished I could have been swimming with them. My feet dangled off the edge of the boat and I could occasionally feel splashes of the ocean. I tried to control my emotions, but tears rolled down my cheeks and onto my dress.

CHAPTER 8

DROWNING

While I was sitting there, I noticed some mangroves nearby. I knew that these patches of trees, roots and vines in the sea were so thick that it was impossible to see through them underwater. They could be breathtaking, but we were headed towards them, and they were getting a little too close for comfort.

"I'm pretty sure there are no dolphins this close to a mangrove," I muttered to myself. I was sure we were going to turn and maybe get a close look at it or something. We kept on moving, closer and closer, until I finally realized we weren't turning. I felt a sudden shock of fear... we were going to crash. I turned around on top of the rail and saw Nelly's head come into view on the stairs. Then suddenly, the whole boat shook and came to a very violent stop. The force pushed me backwards off the railing and off the boat. The last thing that I saw was Nelly's hand reaching out for me.

"Emmi!" Nelly yelled, loud and scared. I screamed at the top of my lungs and moved my hands, trying to grab for something. The world felt like it was moving in slow motion until finally, my back smacked the surface of the water and I was plunged into the cold. I didn't even think about taking a breath or closing my mouth.

The salty water felt like ice against my bare arms. It flooded my mouth and nose and stung my eyes. Instead of trying to stay calm, I struggled to find some way back up. My feet kicked and kicked until my ankle became tangled in an inescapable prison of vines and roots. They were like tentacles that wouldn't let go of me. I couldn't move. I yelled and sobbed, but my voice was drowned out by the frigid water. I was unable to be heard by anyone above the surface.

Water filled my lungs and for the first time, I felt trapped underwater. I couldn't hold my breath anymore. I was too tired to move another muscle. My mind told me to swim back to the surface, to cut through the vines, to block out the haziness that was coming over my eyes, to *breathe*.

I felt myself drifting away when a shadow appeared. I fought to look up. The boat continued to move over my head until the front of it crashed into the mangroves. It was the loudest noise I'd ever heard, even when it was muffled by the water. I closed my eyes when I realized that it didn't matter how long I could hold my breath anymore.

I was drowning.

CHAPTER 9
FLASHBACKS

I don't remember my first time in the water, but my parents described it as magical. I was a toddler on a summer day at the beach. The tide was low, so Mom and Dad decided to see how I would react to the ocean. They sat me just close enough to be touched by the waves. I laughed and screamed with excitement every time the water hit me. I kept trying to move farther out, but Dad would always grab me just in time. After that, they said there was never a day that I didn't want to go to the beach.

In second grade, I was not one of the most-liked kids in school. Everyone thought my friends and I were weird because Nelly wore two different shoes on the first day. (That *tragedy* was how Liz got into fashion.) Anyway, we were taking swimming lessons for gym class one day. We had to get in the pool one person at a time to learn the first steps of swimming. Some of our classmates told Liz, Nelly, and I not to get in the water because we'd probably infect it. (It sounds crazy, but we were in second grade.)

I loved swimming, but no one else knew that. Nelly and Liz were too scared to stand up to the bullies, but I was not going to let someone tell me if I could swim or not. I put on a mean face and when the teacher said the next person could get in, I cut in front of the bullies, jumped in the pool, ignored the teacher, and swam right into the deep end. Because we were in second grade, everyone was super impressed with me and my friends.

We didn't become 'the cool kids' but we weren't 'the weird kids' anymore. I did get in trouble and didn't get a gold star for the day, but I didn't care. My mom didn't either. In fact, she cried after seeing how happy we were not being bullied anymore. We were allowed to have a sleepover on a school night! Swimming helped me make friends.

In fifth grade, my class was doing a science project where we studied the environment on the beach by finding objects and writing down our observations. We had to wear goggles and gloves in case we found anything unsafe, which made us feel more like scientists. Being the nerds of the class, the three of us were taking the assignment seriously. Most of the others weren't.

The teacher told us that if the goggles or gloves got damaged, we would have to pay for them. One of the boys in my class thought it would be funny to take someone else's goggles and throw them in the ocean. So he went up to another boy and did just that. The boy ran after them, but the waves carried the goggles out too far for him to retrieve. He walked back in defeat and told the teacher that he had dropped his. He said that he would pay for new ones because in our minds, snitches were worse than anything.

Everyone was laughing at him, and I thought that was mean. Without thinking, I took off my shoes, gloves, and goggles. I shoved my books into Nelly's arms and ran to the shore. The teacher asked me what I was doing, but I ignored her and dove into the waves. Everyone started chanting my name as I swam against the current and grabbed them. When I swam back, I realized that I had just swum in the ocean fully clothed with seven periods left in the day. My face turned bright red, as I gave the goggles back to the boy. His name was Elliot Peters.

His face turned redder than mine as he thanked me. My teacher's face, however, was the reddest because she was so furious. Without hesitation, she sent me straight to the principal's office. I got detention and dry clothes from the lost and found. Again, my mom wasn't mad. She said I was the nicest and bravest kid in my class.

In my sophomore year of high school, Elliot Peters asked me out on a date. He told me that he had a crush on me ever since I rescued his goggles. I was flattered, and said yes to going out with him. We were together all through high school. Swimming helped me find my first love.

In eighth grade, I invited Nelly and Liz over to swim as often as possible. It wasn't unusual for us to be in the pool the entire day, take a little break, then swim the entire night. We played a variety of games that included relay races, seeing who could make the biggest splash, and who could jump farthest into the pool. We also had contests to see who could hold their breath underwater the longest, and I always won.

One time when we played, I stayed underwater for way longer than normal. Eventually, Nelly and Liz got worried and they tried to pull me up. I waved them away, but they told Mom. The three of them started to pinch me until I came up to breathe. The crazy thing was, I didn't need to. I'd held my breath for so long that I decided to test my ability. Whenever I had free time, I practiced. By the end of grade school, I could hold my breath twice as long as I first thought. Nelly and Liz urged me to post it on social media. Then stories were written about me in newspapers. After that I was on our local news. By the end of my senior year, I had reached a new, seemingly impossible personal record. I felt like I could do anything. Swimming made me feel like a winner.

My freshman year of high school was going terribly. Liz joined cheerleading and was always busy, and Nelly joined every sport she could and never had free time. Even though we were thrown into school with three other classes full of people, I couldn't seem to make friends. So each day after school, I didn't go hang out at a game or a movie; instead, I swam laps.

One Monday after school, I was swimming and didn't hear anyone come in. I checked my stopwatch and my face lit up as I realized I had swum my record time. But then, I heard someone clear her throat. The entire girls' swim team was standing there smiling at me.

"Oh! I'm so sorry. I didn't know you guys were ready to practice."

"Congratulations! You've just made it onto the high school girls' swim team!" announced a senior standing in the front of the group.

"Uh, what?" I asked with skepticism.

"You were amazing! If you swim like that every time you compete, then you would be the fastest swimmer on the team. Would you like to be part of it?" she asked with anticipation in her voice.

"Uh, well, yeah. Sure." I tried to sound calm, but inside I was screaming and jumping up and down with excitement. That's exactly what I did when I got home. My family was so proud of me. As the captain during my sophomore, junior and senior years, our team was one of the best in the state. I even set school records for my individual times. I became more noticed by others in my class and I was moving from 'not weird kid but not cool kid' to 'almost cool kid.' Swimming was now more than a very serious hobby. It was *my* sport. *My* thing. My teammates became my friends and we hung out when we didn't have practice. Nelly and Liz were still my best friends, but when they were busy, I had other people to talk to. I wouldn't have made it through high school if I had been alone much of the time. Swimming filled that void.

The summer after my junior year, my class was having a pool party to celebrate becoming seniors. We rented the public pool for the night and decorated it. We were all having fun swimming when one of the boys started yelling for help. He was in the deep end and appeared to be drowning. Without thinking, I jumped in and dragged him out. He fell to the ground and started choking up water, but he was fine. It turned out that at first he was faking it, so he could get a girl to give him mouth-to-mouth, but then he got a mouthful of water and actually started going under.

Afterwards, Liz and Nelly told me I would be a really good lifeguard, so I got a job at the pool, where I actually did save people from drowning and was named employee of the month. Swimming not only got me a job, but it also helped me save lives.

Then came the summer after I graduated. In one night, everything fell apart. I was in a big fight with my best friends and I was broken up with my boyfriend of three years. Deep down, I knew I was the one who was wrong and that it was all my fault we were fighting. Swimming was all I had left at that moment.

The next day, things got worse. I was involved in a boat crash where I almost drowned. The people I loved were mad at me, and I'd never get the chance to make it right.

CHAPTER 10

WHAT'S WRONG?

I eventually caught my breath and calmed down. I was in the hospital surrounded by my family, Nelly, Liz, and Elliot.

"How are you feeling, sweetheart?" Dad asked. He was sitting next to me with Mom and Liam. Mom was holding my hand, while a tear fell down her cheek.

"Um, better I guess. What happened?" My parents looked at each other. "Why does my ankle hurt so bad?"

"The boat crashed into a mangrove," Mom explained with hesitation. "You fell off. You still have to tell us what happened when you were down there, but the boat went over you." She paused and sniffled back a sob. "You were underwater for so long, Emmi. The rest of us were fine. Only the deck got destroyed. The staff had to send a scuba team underwater to find you. They cut you loose from a terrible tangle of roots and vines. You were unconscious when

47

they brought you to the ambulance." Mom choked up and was drowning in her tears.

She put her trembling hand to her mouth and looked helplessly at Dad. That look reminded me of when my teammates would finish their lap of our relay. They were tired and looking for me to finish off the race. That's what Mom was doing. She was handing off the task to Dad, but he didn't seem like he could do it either.

Dad took a deep breath. "They told us," he paused and cleared his throat awkwardly. "They told us you weren't going to make it."

"But you did make it, and you're going to be okay," Liz jumped in. I managed a small smile. Silence blanketed the room, but everyone's thoughts were the same. They were somehow in shock and filled with joy at the same time.

"So, why does my ankle hurt so bad?"

Once Dad had pulled himself together a little bit more, he said, "You fractured it. The doctors said that you were probably struggling underwater and a vine around your ankle got pulled too tight."

My throat closed up and I swallowed back tears. A fractured ankle? I thought this couldn't get any worse. Then the doctor walked into the room.

"Ah, she's awake!" he said.

"Yeah," I said, not even trying to sound enthusiastic.

"You know, the people who rescued you are *convinced* you can breathe underwater. They are astonished how long you were down there. Okay, everyone, the patient needs some rest. You can come back in and chat later." Everyone said their strained goodbyes.

"Hello, Emiline," he said when everyone had left. I stayed silent as he sat on a stool beside me.

"Well, as you know, your ankle is fractured. You'll need to keep coming back for checkups on that. Your muscles and lungs are very weak, so you'll need physical therapy and breathing treatments." Then he glanced up from his clipboard and looked at me intensely. "Emiline, you are incredibly lucky to be here right now. And with these minor injuries, you will be back to your star swimmer self in no time."

"No!" I yelled, as every muscle in me flinched. The doctor looked startled.

"What's wrong?"

"I-I can't," I said in a shaky voice. He looked at me for a second, then put his clipboard under his arm.

"Hmm," he said. "You don't want to get back in the water?"

I looked down. "I… I can't. No. Not after that… what it did to me. No."

He furrowed his brow and stared at me. My words lingered in the air.

"That is completely normal. You went through something very traumatic and life-altering. The only thing you can do right now is sleep. Then, we can start talking about this."

Although he tried to sound confident, I saw the flicker in his eyes. The flicker of concern as he digested my words. I knew my feelings were not "completely normal."

It seemed like he knew that too.

CHAPTER 11

NIGHTMARE

My chest ached and my head spun, as I slowly sank to the ocean floor. Then…

I opened my eyes and shot up. I looked around and realized where I was. My heart rate gradually slowed down. It was only a dream. No, it was a nightmare. But waking up seemed like a whole new one.

"Emmi, are you okay?" Liz asked, as she looked up from her magazine. My eyes darted over to them when I realized I wasn't alone. Liz was sitting next to Nelly and Elliot.

"Uh, yeah. Yeah, I'm fine. Just a nightmare," I replied a little too enthusiastically. The three of them got up and walked over to me. I tried to relax back into my bed, but it was really uncomfortable.

"How are you feeling?" Liz asked.

"I feel okay. Just a little mushy inside. My ankle doesn't hurt as much."

"That's good," she said. The room became suffocating. Everyone was either looking up or down, not meeting anyone's eyes. All of a sudden, Liz burst into tears.

"We're so sorry!" she cried.

"Liz, don't apologize. You did nothing wrong. I should've just admitted my mistakes from the beginning." Then I looked down at my hands, as my vision got fuzzy. "I wouldn't be in this hospital right now if I would've just admitted that I messed up."

"Let's never fight again," Liz said, as she gave me a tearful hug. When she sat up, Nelly was still standing there, not looking at me.

"I'm going to go get lunch," she said and walked right out of the room. Then Liz asked me a serious question.

"So, are you going to press charges?"

"Press charges? For what?"

"You don't know how the boat crashed?" Liz asked with surprise.

"Well, I guess I didn't really think about it."

Liz chose her words carefully. "The captain fell asleep at the wheel, while we were headed straight towards the mangroves."

"Captain Tracey fell asleep? He would never!"

"It wasn't Captain Tracey. He's on vacation. It was some other guy filling in for him."

"Is he okay?" I asked with concern.

"He's *physically* fine, but he's getting sued by Captiva Dolphin Cruises and he lost his boat license."

"Oh, that must be rough," I said with regret.

"I'll go get the legal papers from your parents. Maybe that'll help you decide," Liz said.

She walked out the door, leaving Elliot and me alone.

CHAPTER 12

NOTHING TO TALK ABOUT

"I'm sorry I got so mad at you," he began. "I did mean most of what I said, but I still overreacted."

I wanted to tell him not to break up with me. I wanted to say that I still had feelings for him. In fact, I remembered the day he asked me to be his girlfriend. I was at my house when I got a text from him.

> **Elliot: Can you come over and help me with something?**
> **Emmi: Sorry, can't. I'm working on my science project.**
> **Elliot: Plz? I really need you right now.**
> **Emmi: I'll call you tonight.**
> **Elliot: It's an emergency! Plz!**

At first, I put down my phone and ignored it. But then, I started to worry that something might be wrong.

What if something really bad happened? It's fine. He'll just call one of his other friends. But he said he needed me. No, I'm busy.

Alas, being a teenage girl with a crush, I caved.

I ditched the science project and texted him. When I got to his house and knocked on the door, his mom answered. She immediately welcomed me in with a huge smile. I was kind of surprised she didn't ask why I was there. I'd only been to Elliot's house with friends. When it was just the two of us, we were either at the beach or out on dates.

"Elliot's in the pool," she said, as she ushered me to the back door.

I walked outside and didn't see anyone. Elliot burst through the surface of the water in the deep end.

"Emmi," he said breathlessly.

"What's the emergency? Is everything okay?"

"Yeah, I'm fine. I just need help finding something." I shot him a confused and annoyed look.

"You need help *finding something?* I drove all the way over here, while your little brother is right inside. Eddy would probably *enjoy* this. Elliot, tell me, how is this an emergency?"

"*It is.* Trust me. Do you have your swimsuit on?"

"Yes, but I'm not helping. I'm going home," I said, as I started walking away.

"No! Emmi, I really need *you* to help. Please?"

Again, I was a teenage girl with a crush, so I caved.

We swam around the deep end looking for whatever Elliot had lost, which made no sense because there was nowhere to lose anything. Every object would've immediately stood out on the pool floor. Then, despite my doubts, I noticed something glimmering in the corner. I dove down a little farther and grabbed it.

"I got something," I said as I broke the surface. We moved over to the edge and sat down.

Elliot peered over my shoulder as I opened my hand. The object turned out to be a necklace. It was a small silver chain with a tiny silver heart pendant. I marveled at its gorgeous simplicity.

"What is this?" I asked, as I looked up at him. That was when I noticed how nervous he'd become.

"This is my way of asking if you'll be my girlfriend," he said shakily. My heartbeat soared, as I comprehended the question.

"Yes," I said through my smile.

"Okay," he said with relief. "I was so nervous." I laughed as he put the necklace around my neck. When he sat back down, he kissed me.

Our very first kiss.

Then I pushed him into the pool and stood up.

"What?" he said when he came up.

"I knew you were being weird. That was a pretty poorly made plan," I joked.

"So you don't want to be my girlfriend?" he teased back.

I rolled my eyes. "I have to go. I'll call you tonight."

Three years ago, I never would've thought that we would have gotten to this point. In one moment, I was holding my beautiful necklace. In the next moment, Elliot and I were faced with a decision that neither of us wanted to make.

"Emmi, can we talk about us?"

"There's nothing to talk about."

"What?" he asked with hurt in his voice.

"Elliot, you don't deserve the way I treated you. I was acting so selfish and didn't even realize that all you wanted was to be with me. You were right. I don't have time for a boyfriend, and that's definitely not going to change now. You need to find someone who will appreciate you."

I never thought the sentence I was about to say would ever come from me. I truly thought he was the person I was going to spend the rest of my life with. But what I told him was true, and I just couldn't handle a relationship. "Let's just be friends, okay?" I finished with a lump in my throat. He stared at me long and hard before he looked down at his hands.

"Um, I guess. If that's what you want." He answered with a blank expression, as if he couldn't process what was happening.

I sat up a little and put my hands behind my neck, feeling for the clasp. I painfully handed back the heart necklace.

"It *is* what I want." He took the necklace and held it up. The chain was slightly rusted and the heart had a little scratch on it.

That tiny scratch suddenly felt as if it were on my real heart.

Elliot and I looked at each other and tried to smile, but it was to no avail.

"I should get going. I really hope you start to feel better," he said, as he pretended he was fine.

"Thanks," I whispered.

When he was gone, my smile fell. I had a feeling his did too.

CHAPTER 13

GRATEFUL

I was lying in my hospital bed looking through documents about the accident. There were *so* many pages. I felt like I'd been reading forever, but was getting nowhere. I still had no clue if I was going to press charges yet. It was all too complicated for me and my parents.

I slapped the stack of endless boredom on my lap and looked at the ceiling. I had been in the hospital for three days now. My lungs were much stronger and my doctor felt like I was ready to begin physical therapy. I itched to get up and move and interact with people other than my family. I got texts from Liz but nothing from Nelly. The only problem with leaving the comfort of my hospital room was that I didn't want to get in the water. I just knew I couldn't do it. Every time I thought about it, I lost my breath for a split second.

I listened to patients scurrying around outside my door. Some were laughing and some were crying. It was actually kind of depressing, listening to all kinds of emotions in one hallway. Suddenly, someone started talking.

"It's a girl!" a woman screamed between happy sobs. I guessed it was a new grandmother.

"Alright!" said a man. He sounded younger and I guessed he was the new father. There was laughter and occasional yelps of joy. I heard their footsteps fade as they walked away. I smiled and shifted to my side, fidgeting with the edge of my pillow.

A moment later I heard slow, heavy footsteps walking towards my door. They stopped for a second and I heard a man clear his throat. Someone else stood up from a chair.

"Is he okay?" the voice asked. It sounded like a young woman who was losing hope. Then there was a pause, as I heard the first footsteps continue to walk towards her.

"Oh, my God!" she whispered in shock. "Oh, my God!" she said louder. Then there was crying. A tear fell down my cheek; it sounded as if she had lost someone she loved.

I turned and sat up in bed. I quickly wiped my eyes. A couple more minutes under that boat, and everyone I loved would have sounded like that grieving lady.

I was tired of feeling sorry for myself. I was going to get up, I was going to start therapy, and I was going to be grateful.

I told myself I could do it, as I ignored the fact that it was suddenly hard to breathe.

CHAPTER 14

YOU GOT THIS?

I was so glad when Mom came to the hospital and dropped off some clothes. I couldn't *wait* to get out of my hospital gown. As soon as she shut the door behind her, I pushed the covers off my lap. I never noticed how cold it was in my room when I was bundled in blankets, but now I shivered. The only time I had gotten up in the past three days was to eat and use the bathroom.

Even though it was hard to move around a lot with my weakened body and ankle, I was getting bored lying around all day. I also felt so disgusting because I woke up every morning with beads of sweat running down my face. It was gross, but it was the closest I got to water. I refused to shower. I told the doctors that it was because it hurt too much to stand for too long, and even though that was true, the main reason was because just looking at water terrified me. I was desperately hoping the therapy would help me with that, even though it didn't make any sense why it would.

I put my feet over the edge of the bed and looked down at them. My right foot had a bright orange fuzzy sock on it. My left one had a black brace that started right below my calf and ended right before my toes. I wiggled them and instantly felt blood start to flow. I shook my head at the tingly feeling. My ankle wasn't fractured that badly, so I could manage to hobble around when I needed to without crutches. I leaned over and ripped off my fuzzy sock from the top and threw it in a pile of dirty laundry that Mom forgot to take home. Then I put my hands on the bed behind me and with my feet on the ground, I pushed myself up. I winced and shifted my weight onto my right foot.

My arms surged with soreness from getting up and I rolled my eyes in frustration. I slowly moved to my clothes that were on the floor directly across the room. I had told Mom to put them there, so that I would have to move to get them. I slowly and painfully got dressed; then I stretched. I tried to touch my toes, but I felt a pull so high up that it looked like I was only bending my neck to look down at my feet.

I looked up in the mirror when I finished and wrinkled my nose. I realized the severity of how badly I needed a shower, as I picked at my greasy hair. Worse yet, Mom chose an outfit that *definitely* didn't match or fit. Feeling so uncomfortable made me want to get better, even more than before.

I grabbed my dirty outfit and noticed there was something left in the pile of clothes that she brought. I moved closer and picked it up. It was my favorite bright orange swimsuit. There was a neon pink sticky note on it that I peeled off and read.

YOU GOT THIS.

I sat down on my bed and glared at the note and at the swimsuit I was holding. I tore the paper in half, again and again, until it was in little shreds. I got up and threw them all into the trash can.

Then without thinking, I threw the swimsuit in the trash too.

CHAPTER 15

I DIDN'T WANT TO BUM ANYONE OUT

left physical therapy with a smile on my face. *I was done!* I was walking with little pain. I had been in therapy for two weeks. At the beginning, it felt like I'd aged 50 years. But, with all of the stretches, exercises, and diet changes, I'd managed to feel somewhat better.

Even with all of the progress I'd made, one problem lingered. I was still too scared to get in the water. From the moment I woke up, the mere thought of it paralyzed me. It was terrifying; it was my new worst fear.

This new fear came with a multitude of consequences. One of them being that I wasn't as clean as I used to be. The most showering I could do was scrub myself with a damp cloth. I had gotten to the point where I was itching all over and couldn't take it anymore. Whenever I tried to take a shower, I would go to the bathroom and just stare for ten minutes. When I could summon some strength, I would extend a trembling hand towards the handle and turn it ever so slightly. As soon as a drop came out, I panicked and shut it off. I would sink to my knees and cry, yelling at myself for being so scared. But I just couldn't bring myself to do it.

I shook the memory out of my mind. I would deal with water later.

Now, I was on my way to the hospital lobby to meet my family and Liz. We were *going out* for lunch. I was giddy with the knowledge that I would be eating something other than cafeteria food. I had texted Nelly, too, but she said she was "busy" and nothing more. I'd seen Liz a couple times since the accident, but I hadn't seen Nelly at all.

I turned the corner and was taken aback when Liz instantly embraced me and asked question after question that she never gave me time to answer. She had been doing this every time that I'd seen her the past two weeks.

"Hey, Liz," I said, when I could breathe.

"Are you ready to get some food?" she asked.

"You have no idea how much I want some Bubble Room right now."

The Bubble Room was a restaurant on Captiva Island that was filled with memorabilia and decorated for Christmas year-round. Colors of the rainbow and multicolored bubbles highlighted the outside walls. It was so unlike any-thing else that it was actually pretty famous.

"Hey, sweetie!" Mom said, as she gave me a hug. Dad and Liam were behind her.

"How do you feel?" Liam asked, as we made our way out of the lobby.

"Physically, I feel so much better." I had to stress that I only felt good physically so that they wouldn't ask if I was ready to swim. That conversation was always so awkward and sad, and I didn't want to bum anyone out.

As we walked to the car, Liz turned to me.

"Emmi, you stink," she said with a disgusted look on her face.

"Alright, Liz, might as well just put it all out there," I said sarcastically.

"Okay, you also don't look very presentable. Please tell me you got dressed in the dark this morning," she said, mo-tioning to my feet.

"Liz, these are compression stockings. They help the circulation," I said bluntly. "No, I am not wearing them voluntarily."

"Oh, thank goodness," she said with relief. I gave her a look and she quickly said, "No, it's not good that you have to wear them. I meant-"

"I'm kidding!" I laughed.

CHAPTER 16

STRANGELY
SERIOUS

While we were driving to the hospital after lunch, I got a message from one of my doctors.

Dr. Gracelynn: Emiline, when you come back to the hospital to clear out your belongings, could you stop by my office? We need to discuss something important.

"I don't feel good," Liam complained, as he sank in his seat.

"I warned you about ordering the adult portion," Dad chuckled from the wheel. "I can't believe you ate all of that."

"So," I interrupted, "I got a message from Dr. Gracelynn. I need to go to her office and talk about something.

Probably just another lecture about stretching." Out of the corner of my eye, I saw my parents glance at each other.

"What?" I questioned.

"Oh, nothing. She just told us about it. That's all," Mom replied cautiously. Before I could interrogate them any further, we pulled into our normal parking space.

"I'll be back in a minute," I said, as I got out of the car. I walked through the automatic doors and the Florida summer heat was replaced with the chilling hospital air conditioning.

Before going to her office, I stopped at my room. I went straight to the sink and grabbed a washcloth from the cabinet above. Liz's words rang through my mind and although I wasn't going to take a shower yet, I didn't want people to cringe at the sight and smell of me. I wet the cloth and scrubbed myself until the washcloth turned brown.

Dr. Gracelynn was definitely one of my favorite people at the hospital. Whenever she walked into my room and found me crying (which I did a lot), she knew exactly how to comfort me. When I was bored and no one was visiting me, we played cards or *Candy Land* on my bed. She always made sure not to sugarcoat any news about my recovery. I was going to miss her the most when I left.

"Hello," I said, as I walked into her office.

"Hi," she replied professionally. I shut the door behind me and sat in the chair across from her. She didn't have her usual bright smile and understanding eyes. Instead, she looked strangely serious.

"What?" I asked. Instead of answering, she slid a brochure across the desk. I flipped it around and read the title. I didn't even need to open it to know what she wanted to talk about.

Sanibel Psychology Associates.

CHAPTER 17

WHY WOULD I NEED TO DO THAT?

My sense of hearing depleted as I stared at the brochure. I sat completely still, while the world spun around me.

"Emmi? Can you hear me?"

"Ialreadydidtherapy," I sputtered in one breath, as I stood up.

"What?" Dr. Gracelynn asked, startled. I closed my eyes and slowly sat back down.

"I just finished therapy," I repeated, trying to sound as normal as possible. I didn't look normal, though. My face had turned pale and I was sweating from every pore.

"Emmi…" she said, as she shifted in her chair. "This isn't *physical* therapy. You'll be meeting with a psychologist."

"Why would I need to do that?"

I didn't understand why those words were coming out of my mouth. I knew I needed help. To put it plainly, I had *so* many problems. I didn't know exactly what was going on with me, but I wanted it to be over. So why was I being so defensive?

She seemed to sense these thoughts, so she stopped talking calmly and stared me dead in the eyes.

"Emiline, when do you plan on starting to swim again?"

I broke eye contact and looked back at the brochure.

"I don't know. I thought I'd take a break."

"What about your swim meet next Saturday? I noticed you were cleared for it."

"No."

"What about your job at the aquarium?"

"I quit a few days ago."

"Did you tell anyone?"

"No."

"What about that commercial? Are there any more scenes you need to be in?"

"I don't know."

"Is the pool at your house going to be used soon?"

"Please, stop…"

"When was the last time you drank a bottle of water?"

"Stop!" I screamed.

She blinked in total shock and disappointment. I stared at her for a long moment, surprised at my own intensity.

Then I left.

CHAPTER 18
HOP IN

I ran out the back door of the hospital and collapsed on a bench. People stared at me because I was crying, but I didn't care. I wanted to leave before my family could find me. I didn't want to talk with them about going to therapy yet.

I called Nelly and, of course, she didn't answer. She hadn't since the day I woke up. Liz rode to the hospital with my family, so she didn't have a car. I thought about calling one of my friends from the Bull Sharks, but they probably would have been freaked out by the fact that I needed to be picked up from the hospital "pronto, no questions." I scanned through my contacts, but I couldn't really explain to anyone else what had happened. Finally, after I searched every name, I went back up to the E's.

That name was my last resort, but he was the only person I could call. I sat there, staring at my phone, trying to come up with any other possible solution. I was running out of time, so finally, I clicked the call button next to his name.

"Hello?" he answered immediately.

"Hi, Elliot," I said, in a weird voice that didn't sound like me.

"Uh… hi. Why- why'd you call?" he asked awkwardly.

"Um, can you come pick me up at the hospital?" I said nervously.

There was a long pause on his end. Then he said, "Okay, yeah, sure."

"Thanks so much."

It only took him about five minutes to arrive, so I got the feeling he drove a little too fast. When he pulled up to where I was sitting and rolled down his window, he said, "Hop in."

I walked briskly to his car. When I got in, I noticed he was staring at me, but I didn't say anything. We sat in silence for a few seconds more, as he kept staring at me and I continued looking straight ahead.

"I'm sorry, but can we go? I kind of want to get home," I said, breaking the ice-cold quiet. Elliot quickly put his hands on the wheel. He started to drive, but then stopped abruptly. "What are we doing?" I said, trying not to let the irritation come through in my voice.

"Emmi, are you doing okay?" He put the car in park, so I tossed the crinkled brochure in his direction. He picked it up and read the front, then looked at the back, then at the front again. "Sanibel Psychology Associates. Are you going into therapy?"

"No," I mumbled, as I looked out my window. I could still feel his troubled gaze on me. But, he knew me better than most people. He understood what I was feeling before I even did. Without any additional comments, he drove away from the hospital and straight to my house.

"Thanks," I said, as he pulled into my driveway. Before I could open the door, the locks clicked shut.

"Emmi, I know you don't *want* to talk about this, but you *need* to." I turned away from the door and finally looked him in the eye. "What are you thinking?"

"I don't know… I understand that being scared of water is not common. Even just saying it sounds ridiculous." He didn't look at me like I was being ridiculous, though. So I continued. "We all thought this was going to pass after a few days of being in the hospital, but it never did. I guess starting therapy is like saying that this is way bigger than we thought it was going to be. That there's something *seriously* wrong with me." I had to look away to stop my tears.

He gathered his thoughts before speaking. "I know this is way different than anything you've ever experienced before. You have a very unusual fear, but nothing is wrong with *you*. It's not your fault this is happening. But, I agree with your doctor."

He put his hand on my chin and turned my head towards his. "The only way you're going to overcome this is by accepting that it's happening and doing everything you can to treat it. Even if it means having to do some things that you never would have imagined. No one is going to think any less of you if you start seeing a therapist. We just want you to be happy again."

A tear rolled down my cheek. He wiped it away with his thumb, before turning back to the brochure.

"Besides," he said as he opened it, "they have a very high success rate. Five stars!" he joked, as he pointed to the page. I couldn't help but laugh.

"Alright," I nodded after a while. "I think I'll do it." He leaned over and hugged me for a long time. Then I asked, "How did you come up with all of that?"

"Why do you think I was silent the whole ride here? I was thinking," he said with a smile. I laughed again.

"Thank you so much," I said, as I started to get out of the car.

"If you ever need anything else, I'm your guy."

He looked at me as if I was his only care in the world. And at that moment, I was.

CHAPTER 19

I WAS FREAKING OUT, OKAY?

I stepped through my front door and took a deep breath. It felt like I hadn't been home in forever. While I was at the hospital, I imagined this moment being the defining point when the chaos would finally be over. I closed the door behind me and reminded myself that it was just the beginning.

My footsteps echoed through the empty house when I walked to my bedroom. It appeared almost exactly how I had left it just a couple weeks earlier. My pajamas were still in a crumpled heap in the middle of the floor. The medal I had gotten from our first swim meet was lying on the dresser. I had hastily set it there, instead of hanging it up with the others. As I made my way towards it, I remembered the exhilaration of winning. I relived cutting through the water and beating the girls beside me.

And I felt content with never doing that again.

The only things that were different about my room were that the dresser drawers were closed and my bed was made, undoubtedly by Mom. I imagined her not knowing what to do with herself when she was waiting for me to get better. I could almost see her pacing footprints on the soft carpet. Her fingerprints on my covers were almost traceable.

I sighed, as I turned from the corkboard where my medals were hanging and threw myself on the bed. Even though I knew it was irresponsible to leave the hospital without telling anyone, I still didn't text my family. I wanted to enjoy my privacy before they bombarded me with angry lectures and pitying questions about therapy. So, I changed into clean clothes and waited for them to get home.

Hour after hour ticked by, as I waited for the front door to open. By then I had started to become worried where they were. I was so conflicted with my decision to stay quiet that I kept picking up my phone, then setting it back down again. Finally, I opened up my messages and started to type, when I heard the door downstairs open.

I heard footsteps in the kitchen but there was no talking. The only other noises were the clinking of keys being dropped on the counter, running water, clanking pots, and a character on TV, who was talking in a cartoonish voice. Everything seemed completely normal. There was no mention of me and no one came upstairs to see if I was okay. After a while, there was some faint chit-chat that I couldn't make out, even with my ear pressed against my door.

I checked all my social media, cleaned my room, did some college research, and watched several YouTube videos. I also took another look at the papers on Captain Benny. I'd read it all, yet I still hadn't made a decision. I had just set them down when finally, a voice came from the kitchen.

"Emmi, dinner is ready and we made spaghetti," Mom yelled. I sat up in bed and looked at my door, as if I was trying to see through it and see what they were planning. *How did they know I was here? Why didn't they say anything to me?* I brushed off my questions and decided to go eat anyway. I had been trying not to acknowledge the constant grumbling of my stomach, but I couldn't bear the hunger anymore.

I twisted my door handle and pushed it open. When I was met by the aroma of food, I took the steps a little faster. When I got to the bottom, I could see everyone sitting at the dinner table. There was small talk about my brother going to his friend's house the next day. I stepped slowly through the kitchen, grabbed a plate from the cupboard and poured a glass of juice. My pulse raced even more, as I carried them to the table.

When I set my plate and glass down and scooped some spaghetti, I finally looked up to see them all looking back.

"Hi."

Mom smiled at me uncomfortably. "Hi, honey. How are you feeling?"

"Fine."

Liam was eating his food slower than usual, occasionally looking up at me. Mom was nodding and smiling at everyone. Each time she took a bite, she muttered, "Mmm." Dad was trying his best to act normal, but he wasn't doing a great job at it. You could tell he was angry because he was stabbing at his food. I couldn't take it anymore.

"Okay, stop. Just go ahead and yell at me. Get it over with," I said suddenly.

"Alright then, we will," Dad said, slamming down his fork.

Mom's voice rose when she said, "Tom, we are not going to yell at her."

"Yes, Bethany, we are," he answered in anger.

"I'm sorry for running out of the hospital without telling you where I was going. I know that was completely inconsiderate," I said quickly.

"If Elliot had not texted us, you would be in deeper trouble," Dad exclaimed. (I should've known that Elliot would tell them.)

"I understand your meeting with Dr. Gracelynn was probably hard, but why did you run away?" Mom asked.

"Because, *Mom*, I have to see a *therapist*. Like, a *full-on psychologist*. It wasn't exactly easy to hear that I was going crazy!"

"Emiline!"

"At the time, I didn't feel like talking about it with you guys." Liam looked at me, offended. "I was freaking out, okay?" I closed my eyes and took a deep breath. "But that doesn't matter now. I've decided to do it." Everyone looked at me in shock.

"Okay, that's great," Dad said with uncertainty.

"Yes, I think this will help so much," Mom said. She stood up and kissed the top of my head. "I'll call the office tomorrow."

"But, please don't run away again," Dad said with authority.

"I'm so sorry. I won't. I promise."

A few minutes passed, as we started eating again. Then, Mom looked up and said, "You know who you really need to apologize to? Your doctor."

My eyes widened, as I left to message Dr. Gracelynn.

What a way to say goodbye.

CHAPTER 20

A PERFECT PERSON

"Mom, you just missed your turn again," I said, as I looked up from the GPS on my phone.

"Sorry!" she yelled. The GPS rerouted again. Five extra minutes.

It was the day of my first therapy session. I had wanted to go by myself, but Mom had insisted on taking me.

The company where my therapist worked was in Sanibel, so it was about a 30-minute drive. It was sort of inconvenient, but Dr. Gracelynn had said that Dr. Marshal was excellent, especially in working with teenagers.

Mom's frustration grew, even though we would still be arriving ten minutes before my appointment. Frankly, I was glad she'd missed the turn again.

"Come on, let's hurry," she said as we parked. I got out of the car and shaded my eyes. I looked up at the building where I would be spending every Monday morning from eight to nine o'clock.

I didn't know what I had expected the place to look like, but that was not it. The property was surprisingly very beautiful and serene. The parking lot was gravel instead of pavement and there were large orange and pink flower bushes in front of the massive white building. There were pillars that went from the porch to the teal blue roof. What really caught my eye was the sign that had an open clam shell on the left with the words "Sanibel Psychology Associates" on the right.

Then I remembered it was my therapist's office, and it started to look like a prison again.

"Name?" asked the lady at the front desk.

"Ganson," Mom answered.

"You can take a seat. Dr. Marshal is finishing up a session."

We made our way over to the waiting room and sat down. There were a few other people there, but I didn't acknowledge them. I was so nervous that if I looked at anything but my shoes, I felt sick. My leg was bouncing so fast that my whole body moved with it. Mom occasionally said something, but I never answered. I was afraid that if I talked, I would cry. After about ten minutes, someone walked into the lobby.

"Emiline?"

I jolted and Mom quickly stood up. The woman smiled, not surprised with our reaction, and continued. "Hello, my name is Dr. Marshal."

"Hi!" Mom said cheerfully, as she reached out to shake her hand. "I'm Bethany."

Then I realized I was still sitting down, so I jumped up faster than Mom had. When the chair squeaked, everyone in the room turned to look at me.

Dr. Marshal met my eyes. "You must be Emiline. Follow me and we'll go to my office."

She and Mom started walking away, but I stood still. When Mom noticed that I hadn't moved, she turned around, put her hand on my back and guided me down the hall.

The office was exactly like the ones in the movies. In my opinion, it was bigger than necessary for just two people. At one end of the room was a small kitchen and a door to the bathroom. In the opposite corner, there was a tidy desk with a large computer monitor sitting in the middle. Across from the desk were two long couches that faced each other. The room was lit by natural light coming in from two windows that nearly took up the whole wall. I thought it looked really nice, until I reminded myself once more that I was trapped.

"You can sit down. I need to talk to your mother and then we can begin," Dr. Marshal said, as she pointed at a couch. I nodded and they left the room.

I slowly walked over and gingerly sat down. The cushions were comfortable, but I didn't relax. I was still so nervous that I suddenly had the urge to leap through the window and drive myself home. I wouldn't have been sitting in that office if it weren't for Elliot. I agreed with everything he had said, yet I still hated myself for listening to him.

Suddenly, the door started to open. My heart dropped and I felt tears sting my eyes. *Stop acting like a four-year-old.*

"Okay," Dr. Marshal said, as she closed the door behind her. She walked over to her desk, picked up a clipboard and a pen, continued walking to the couch across from me, and sat down.

"Emiline, you can call me Jess. Do you go by anything besides Emiline?"

I shrugged.

Then she looked at me with determination. "First of all, before every session, I want you to have a list of things that happened during the week. This way, we can make sure nothing is forgotten."

As she handed me an orange spiral notebook, she added, "Secondly, I think that if you see me as a friend, it'll be easier to open up. So, I'm 26 years old and I'm originally from Indiana. I'm also engaged to my fiancé, Jeremy."

She continued to talk, but I zoned out. Dr. Marshal had short, light-brown hair that shaped her face. Her hazel eyes were shining behind clear-framed glasses. She was wearing some makeup, but she obviously didn't need it. She was also very tall and very thin and had a great sense of fashion. She was young, intelligent, beautiful, kind, and engaged. So basically, she was perfect.

But that was how therapy worked, right? A perfect person treated an imperfect person.

I shifted on the couch and tried to listen. "I know it can be hard to talk about these things. This trauma you've experienced is incredible. But I'm only here to help you." Then she switched from intense to calm. "So, let's get started. Can you give me an overview of what you've been doing and how you've been feeling since you got home?"

A million different answers filled my head, yet I didn't talk. I just looked at her and watched as her patient expression changed to one of confusion.

"Sorry, did you hear me?" she asked politely. I nodded. My leg started to bounce again. "Can you please answer my question? I need to know what you've been doing and how you've been feeling since you got home."

Again, I just looked at her. *Why am I not speaking?*

She tilted her head slightly and said, "Okay, we'll move on."

She stood up and walked over to her desk. When she returned to the spot where she'd been sitting, she held a piece of lined paper in front of her and started to read.

"Two billion people in the United States visit the ocean every year."

I started to sweat. *Two billion? They need to stop. That's so many people in danger. That's so many people. They could end up like me!*

"Seventy-one percent of the Earth's surface is water."

Almost immediately, it felt as if all of the oxygen had been sucked out of the room. *Seventy-one percent? That means there's only twenty-nine percent of the world left. It's everywhere. Where am I supposed to go?*

"Sixty percent of the human body is made of water."

Everything started to itch. *It's taking over me!* I tried to look normal, but I couldn't hide my anxiety. I pushed on my leg, then rubbed my hands together, then rubbed my arms until finally, I had to speak.

"Stop!" I screamed. I started to cry, so I picked up a pillow and wiped my tears.

"Oh, Emiline! I'm so sorry," she said, as she sat next to me and wrapped her arms around me.

"I can't live like this!" I cried into her shoulder. "It almost drowned me! It almost killed me! But I can't get away from it. I'm so scared!" I started crying so hard that I could barely understand myself.

Somehow, she calmed me down. I didn't know what she said, or if she said anything at all. But in ten minutes, we

were facing each other on my couch with a plate of cook-
ies between us. Pretending like nothing had happened, she
asked me to talk about my family and friends.

I hesitated, but I decided I had to say *something*. I told
her about Mom, who did everything to make our family
happy. Dad, who could cheer us up no matter what. Liam,
who was the kindest and most understanding person I'd ever
met. Liz, who knew me better than anyone in the world.
And Nelly, who always pushed me to be the best version of
myself. I left Elliot out because I didn't really know what he
meant to me anymore. I even told her how I'd felt when I
thought I was never going to see them again…

When I finished talking 40 minutes later, she moved
back over to her couch. "I've learned a lot about you today,
Emiline. But one crucial detail I picked up on is that you
value family more than anything else." She paused and stared
into my eyes. "I can help you. I *know* you can get through this
fear. But the only way this is going to work is if you communicate with me and listen to me. Do you understand?"

I nodded, then I quickly said, "Yes."

She paused for a long moment before she spoke. "I
think I have a strategy to get you showering again." *I never
told her I wasn't showering? Oh. She could probably tell.*

As she explained her plan, doubts crept back into
my mind.

"Emiline?"

"Yes?"

"You have to try it. It might sound hopeless to you, but I think it might work." I nodded and swallowed a lump in my throat. Then she looked down at her watch. "Alright, it's nine. I'll see you next week." We both stood up and she gave me a hug.

As I walked out the door, I said, "Thank you, Dr. Marshal."

"Please, call me Jess," she said with a smile.

"And you can call me Emmi."

CHAPTER 21

LA LOO LA LEE

"**A**re you almost ready?" Liam asked impatiently.

I shot him a glare. "Hold on."

My first therapy session had been filled with ups and downs. Despite my resistance to participate, Jess had somehow hatched a plan to make showering possible. Her theory was that as long as I was constantly reminded that my family was there and that I was not back at the accident site, I would be okay. I was *very* skeptical. It just seemed way too simple. But, she had insisted that I listen to her.

It was the Sunday before my next appointment and I still hadn't showered. I had been putting it off the whole week. I even waited until Thursday to tell my family the plan. As I had expected, they kept badgering me about it until I finally gave in. I just couldn't walk into her office without trying.

Liam and I had been standing in the bathroom for ten minutes.

"I can't do it," I said breathlessly. I put my hands on my head and backed up against the sink.

"Yes, you can."

"No, I can't."

I closed my eyes. I felt the color drain from my face and heard ringing in my ears. Then I felt arms around my waist and a head leaning against my side. Liam was trying to comfort me. He looked sad and nervous because he wanted me to get better more than anything.

I hugged him back and then pulled away. "Do you promise not to leave?" I asked in a quivering voice.

"I'll be right outside the door, talking to you the whole time. I promise." He held my attention for a while longer, giving me even more reassurance. When he left the bathroom, he yelled, "Just concentrate on my voice! La loo la lee!"

Finally, I took a deep breath and turned the faucet handle. I jumped, as the sound of rushing water brought back painful memories. My breathing became shallow. But I had to keep going. I held my hand under the stream to check the temperature. I quickly pulled it back, as the same feeling of reopened wounds shot through me. Then, water unexpectedly splashed the hand I was leaning on. I gasped and picked it up, fell, and hit my chin on the side of the tub. Luckily, it wasn't bad and my lip only bled a little.

"Emmi? Are you okay?" Liam asked from behind the door. I swallowed my yelps of pain. I couldn't let this stop me. I stood up in front of the mirror and saw someone I didn't recognize. *This isn't me. Emmi's not scared to swim. Emmi's not scared to shower. Emmi's not scared of water.* I wiped the back of my hand across the cut. There I stood, trembling, with skin hanging from my lip, a bruised chin, and a broken heart.

Then, somehow, even with all of my doubts, I fought through the bad memories and found the strength to reply.

"I'm getting in now!"

CHAPTER 22

SO EMBARRASSING

"You did it!" Jess said when I walked into her office. The night before, I had showered for the first time in almost a month. After finally being clean, I was able to take my hair out of a messy bun and dress up a little. Even to me, I looked like a completely different person.

"Before we get to anything else that happened this week," she said as I started to open my notebook, "how did it feel to shower again?"

Suddenly, I felt like a twelve-year-old being interrogated by her friends. It felt so silly to be excited over taking a shower. It was just so embarrassing that my life had come to this.

"Liam helped me," I answered bluntly. She waited for me to elaborate, but I didn't.

"Okay," she said slowly. "Can you give me more details?"

"It was... scary." Again, I didn't say more. I looked away from her and tucked my hair behind my ear.

"I know *exactly* what you're thinking," she said with confidence.

"Huh?"

"You're thinking that this fear of yours is something to be embarrassed about." I didn't confirm or deny her accusation, so she continued. "I don't need thirty years of experience to notice a pattern with my clients. At some point during therapy, everyone becomes embarrassed about whatever they're here for and they stop talking to me. Frankly, it's normally not on the second day. Although, I'm not surprised. You seem very stubborn."

"Hey-"

"But, I always help them realize that there is nothing to be ashamed of. Everyone has struggles. You're just one of the few who are brave enough to admit it. So, again, I'm telling you that all I'm here to do is help you. Nothing you could ever say will make me judge you. So let's try this again. How did you feel when you touched water?"

I took a deep breath and finally decided to trust her.

"Well, I waited until last night to try and shower. First of all, I slipped and fell. That's where I got this," I said, pointing to my bruised chin. Jess nodded with raised eyebrows and I continued. "When I first got in, my whole mind kind of froze... I guess?" I squinted as I tried to explain.

"I didn't remember much. The only thought I had was that I... I was drowning."

I paused for a moment, then cleared my throat. "But Liam sat outside the bathroom door, talking to me the whole time. When I heard his voice, I remembered where I really was and what was really happening. I don't even remember what he said. I just knew I was ultimately going to be okay."

Jess just looked at me with a soft smile.

"But that doesn't mean I'm showering every single day. Or even every two days."

She burst into laughter. "Okay, Emmi. That's fine with me."

CHAPTER 23

UM, LUNCH ON US?

After I had encountered water for the first time since the accident, Jess encouraged me to try simple things like drinking water. I had been staying hydrated by everything other than water, and I was *so* sick of it. But, anything was better than consuming the thing that almost *killed* me.

A few weeks after my first shower, Liz and I were hanging out at the Bubble Room for lunch.

"Do you girls each want to start with some water?" the waiter asked when he came over to our table. Liz and I made eye contact as soon as he said "water." Only, she was smiling and I was frowning. We looked back at the waiter.

"Yes!" Liz said.

"No, thank you," I said at the same time.

Without my consent, Liz said, "Sorry about her. Yes, we would like water. Two please." He nodded, jotted it down on his notepad and left.

"You're doing it today. You're drinking water!" she said with enthusiasm, flipping her brown hair behind her shoulders. She was excited, while I had a pit in my stomach.

"Liz, I can't do it. Not yet."

"Don't say that!" she replied a little too loudly. Heads turned in our direction.

Great. If people recognized me from newspapers, drinking water would be even harder. As soon as the thought popped into my head, I knew it was too late. Some adults started whispering to each other, while children whined to know what they were talking about. I put my face in my hands.

"I can't do it, Liz!" She looked at me for a moment, wiggling her eyebrows like this was a joke. She pushed herself away from the table and stood on her chair, as the waiter came out with our water.

"Liz! What are you doing?" I said through clenched teeth.

Now people were *really* staring. She cleared her throat before addressing everyone.

"Attention!" she announced with her hands cupped around her mouth. "You may already know this young lady sitting across from me; her name is Emiline Ganson. Long story short, she fell off a boat, almost drowned and is now scared of water."

"That's an understatement," I mumbled. Liz gave me a dirty look and put a finger to her lips. I sank a little more in my chair.

"But today is the day that Emmi will overcome another obstacle. She will drink water for the first time since the crash!"

She had everyone's full attention, so she hopped off her chair, took the glasses of water right out of the waiter's hands, and set one down right in front of me. I looked at it, then back at her.

"I mean it, Liz!"

"Emmi, all of these people want you to do it. I believe in you."

She looked at me so ecstatically that it was annoying. To add more pressure, everyone in the restaurant, now knowing my story, was smiling at me.

I huffed and sat up in my chair. Because there was so much attention on me, I tried not to let my fear show. The truth was, it felt like that overwhelming moment when I was standing in front of the shower. My heart pounded.

"Oh, alright, fine!" I said with disgust. I reached for the glass and brought it to my mouth. When I felt the cold condensation on my hand, I almost dropped it, but I didn't. I took a small sip and then a large gulp. Then I set it down and quickly wiped my hand on my shorts.

"Yes!" Liz screamed. She came around the table and embraced me. Everyone else clapped and cheered. The waiter, still confused, smiled awkwardly.

"Um, lunch on us?" he asked.

While we were eating, people we didn't know congratulated me. The whole restaurant seemed to become louder and more excited. By the time I had finished my food, my whole glass of water was empty.

When Liz and I were walking to the car, something strange occurred to me.

"Do you know what you just did?" I asked seriously.

"I just stood up in front of a whole restaurant and demanded *strangers* to listen to me. I know! That was so unlike me!"

I kept a blank face. "Yeah, actually. It was unlike you. It was like *Nelly*."

"What?"

"You forced me into doing something that you knew would be good for me. She's not here, so without even realizing it, you're doing something she would've done."

"That's ridiculous!"

"Liz, where's Nelly?"

Her smile slowly disappeared.

"I'm sorry, Emmi, but it's not my tale to tell. All I can say is that she is going through something that I could not imagine going through myself. If you want an explanation, she needs to be the one to give it to you."

I didn't know how to respond. *What in the world could she be going through that was worse than what I was going through?* I immediately felt guilty.

I started walking away from her and said, "Okay. Thanks for helping me earlier, I guess."

We drove all the way home without speaking.

CHAPTER 24

MOM'S GRAND GESTURE

"**A**re you sure about this?"

"*Yes*, Tom. One hundred percent. I *am* her mother. It will be so much fun."

I am her mother. She is my daughter. It will be fun. It will be good for her. Listen to me. Those were just a handful of phrases that Mom had been using the entire week after she had hatched her plan. She decided it would be a brilliant idea to have the Rhymes and the Millers over for brunch.

Obviously, our families had put Sunday morning dolphin watches on hold. We had communicated a little by text, but other than that, we hadn't all met together since the crash.

When Mom announced that we would be hosting brunch at our house, Liam was ecstatic. Dad had the opposite reaction, though. He stared at her like he was going to explode. As for my reaction, I felt a little like Dad on the inside, but when I saw how happy Mom was, I tried to look like Liam on the outside. I gave a weak, no-teeth smile and said, "Cool."

Despite how Dad felt, Mom started planning. She texted the Moms, made a menu, sent out a dress code, got out the yard games and bought all of the supplies she needed.

The closer it got to Sunday, I honestly didn't want the get-together at all.

"Bethany, I will tell you what I've been telling you ever since you came up with this idea. Do you realize what we are doing? We are reenacting the worst day of our lives!" he said urgently as I listened at the bottom of the stairs.

There. That was how I felt.

"We are not! We are simply having a nice meal with our friends." Then her voice softened. "Tom, she needs this. She had to quit the swim team, she hasn't talked to anyone from school, she broke up with Elliot, and I feel like she and Nelly aren't getting along. I just want to make sure she knows she's loved."

And that was why I needed to go along with her plan, no matter how uncomfortable it might be. I knew how she felt. She was just trying to help. This was Mom's grand gesture to show she cared.

When I explained the brunch to Jess, she felt that the whole thing was questionable. Not because it would trigger anything in me, but for the same reasons Dad had. Then, she beat me to explaining why Mom was having brunch in the first place.

It was the first time that she and I had agreed on something so quickly.

By the time that dreaded Sunday morning arrived, I had to disguise my true feelings. When the oven timer beeped loudly, I reluctantly made my way down the steps.

"Good morning!" Dad said with a smile, as I walked over and gave him a hug.

"Good morning. Everything smells great, Mom."

"Thanks!" she replied, as she took the steaming breakfast casserole out of the oven and set it on the counter.

As hungry as I was, even I could admit that she'd made *way* too much food. There was a casserole, muffins, pancakes, waffles, three types of eggs, bacon, sausage links, cinnamon rolls, orange juice, coffee, bagels, donuts, and gluten-free waffles. I didn't think there was even a gluten-free person in any of the families.

"Tom, can you make the fruit salad?" she asked, as she pulled homemade cinnamon roll icing out of the fridge. He nodded and started towards the mound of assorted fruit.

"Emmi, you look so nice! Can you go check on your brother? I told him to change his clothes twenty minutes ago."

"Yep."

When I opened his door, he was sitting on his bed, still wearing his *Captain America* shirt and eating a chocolate muffin.

"What are you doing?" I asked with a smirk.

"Nofen," he said with a mouthful of muffin.

"Did Mom give you that?"

"No way. I took it when she wasn't looking. I hate waiting this long to eat. I'm so hungry!"

"That is the entire point of brunch," I laughed, as I took it out of his hand and broke off a piece for myself. "It's okay. I don't get it either. Anyway, you have to get changed. The Rhymes and the Millers are going to be here soon. Did Mom pick out your clothes?" He nodded and pointed at the white polo and khakis hanging on his door knob.

"Well, she wasn't thinking straight. There is no way you're wearing a white shirt, while Jack and the twins are here."

I started rummaging through his closet when he said, "I'm *so* excited! Are you?"

He hadn't had a single friend over the whole summer. My parents didn't want to explain to them why they couldn't swim. At first, I thought it was ridiculous, but I think they had talked to Liam about it soon after I got home. He eventually became okay with it, but he definitely missed having friends over.

"Sure, I'm excited," I mumbled.

Just as I pulled a darker polo out of his closet, the doorbell rang.

"They're here!"

CHAPTER 25
SORRY WE'RE LATE

The Rhymes arrived in a bustle of greetings. Liam flew out the door to the twins, while the rest of us hugged. My parents helped carry things into the house and I walked in beside Liz.

"Hey," she said, as I took a box of donuts out of her arms.

"Hey." We walked in and stopped in the foyer.

"Emmi, is this weird for you? Because it is for me. It's like we are purposely reminding each other why we aren't doing Sunday morning brunch anymore."

"Believe me, I know. But Mom was so excited to see everyone; I didn't want to ruin it. I think I'll be fine, but it'll be a little strange." I was trying to convince myself of this as much as I was trying to convince her.

"Okay," she said, while putting an arm around my shoulders. Then we walked into the kitchen to see a cloud of smoke on the ceiling.

"Mom!"

"Yes?" She turned her head from the conversation in the living room. "Oh no!" She ran over and opened the oven. It emitted another huge dark cloud that went right in her face.

"What is it?" Dad asked, while hurrying over.

"The bacon is burnt," she said through her coughing. As she set the tray on the stove, the side of it hit the edge of the waffle plate. It catapulted the whole pile of waffles either into the burnt bacon grease or on the floor.

"It's alright," Mr. Rhymes said. "There's plenty of food. We'll help you clean."

Mom apologized over and over. I knew we had food to spare, but why did it have to be the bacon?

It had officially been a half-hour since the Millers were supposed to show up. Everything was clean, the table had been set, Liam and the twins were called into the house and then let back outside again. The rest of us were sitting in the living room. One thing I noticed was that we were only talking about what the Rhymes had going on. Mom and Dad hadn't done much all summer besides worry about me, and no one was ready to talk about that yet.

"Should we text them?" Dad wondered ten minutes later. As soon as he finished his sentence, the doorbell rang. We all stood up simultaneously, while Mom rushed over to welcome them.

When she opened the door, there stood the Millers. Well, most of them. Mr. and Mrs. Miller both had tired eyes and forced smiles. Mom faltered but reached over to give them hugs anyway.

"Hello, Laney! How are you, John?"

"Sorry we're late," Mr. Miller said, as he set a pitcher of lemonade on the counter. While they all continued to say their hellos to Tommy and Jack, I noticed someone was missing.

"Where's Nelly?" I blurted from the living room. Everyone stopped talking and looked at Mrs. Miller. She glanced at her husband before addressing all of us.

"Penelope doesn't feel well. She couldn't get out of bed this morning." The words sounded rehearsed. Jack looked at his mom, confused, but shrugged it off. While everyone started visiting, Tommy walked over to me and Liz.

"More like she *wouldn't* get out of bed this morning."

"What?" I asked.

"She's not sick. She just refused to come."

I looked over at Liz, who was staring into space with a sad expression. I rolled my eyes. Even though I hadn't expected Nelly to show up, it still hurt all the same.

"Can someone go get Liam and the girls?" Liz's mom asked.

"I will," Tommy volunteered. When he left, the conversation dropped off. Someone said the food smelled great and another said the house looked nice.

"So, Emmi, how's everything going?" Mr. Miller asked. Everyone looked my way.

"Oh, um, okay, I guess." They all nodded. For a moment, they all seemed thankful that I didn't elaborate.

"Hey, let's hope this brunch goes better than the last one!" he joked awkwardly. Everyone's eyes got wide and his wife turned to reprimand him.

"John!"

"Sorry! Sorry!"

"A little too soon," Dad mumbled. Liz put her hands on her head.

"It's fine," I said, desperately trying to save the meal. Just then, Tommy burst into the house with Melissa in his arms.

"She fell off the playhouse and hurt her leg," he shouted, over her cries.

"Oh, no!" Mrs. Rhymes hurried over. "It's really swelling." Melissa cried louder.

Dad gave her an ice pack and when she put it on Melissa's leg, she screamed.

"Honey, what do you want us to do?" After five minutes of more crying, Mom finally asked what we were all thinking.

"Catherine, do you need to take her home? Or to the doctor?" Mrs. Rhymes looked desperately at her husband.

"Probably," he said with worry.

"I'm so sorry," she said, as she started to pick up her daughter.

"It's totally fine. You need to make sure she's okay," Mom said. Even though she tried not to show it, she sounded devastated.

"She's so dramatic," Liz muttered. "I guess I'll text you later?"

"Yeah, that's fine. See ya."

"We should probably go too; we might as well reschedule?" Mrs. Miller asked, as the crying continued.

"Oh, yes! We'll just get together when everyone can be here," Mom said with even more disappointment when she walked them out.

We would definitely not be rescheduling.

The rest of the day, Mom boxed up the breakfast food that we would be eating for the next couple of weeks. We all stayed to ourselves, not wanting to do anything. Around eight o'clock, I was watching a movie in the living room when I heard my parents on the back porch.

"What are you guys talking about?"

"Oh, just about how huge of a disaster this morning was," Mom said sarcastically.

"I'm sorry it went so wrong. You put a lot of work into it," I sympathized.

"Well, I probably deserved it. I should've listened to your father. I told myself I was doing it for you and that it would make you feel better. The truth is, I was really only doing it for myself. I felt so useless and I just needed to do something to make me feel like I was helping you."

I reached for her hand. "Mom, we all knew how you felt. But you can't just fix this whole fear of water like it's a regular emotion. You both are helping me so much, but I will be the one who finally overcomes it."

"You're doing just fine, sweetheart," Dad said, as Mom wiped her eyes.

"Ugh! Okay, I'll back off," she joked.

A few moments later, Dad brought up something that was bothering him. "By the way, Emmi, I'm sorry about what John said earlier. That was so childish."

I laughed. "No, it's fine. He only said what we were all thinking."

CHAPTER 26

IMMATURE

I had been doing the same thing every night since I got home from the hospital: watching movies, eating ice cream, and looking over the accident papers.

I was rapidly turning each wrinkled page of the packet in frustration. The due date for my decision was coming up and I was getting nowhere. There was so much information in the packet, yet nothing helped me. The pages only told the same story I already knew. Captain Tracey was on vacation and when Captain Benny filled in for him, he fell asleep, while steering the boat and crashed it. When questioned, Benny told them he had been extremely tired and that it was an accident. I just couldn't make a decision. Every time I read his story, I had a sinking feeling that there was something I didn't know.

There was a picture taken of him prior to the accident that was paper clipped to the pages. He had dark brown, graying hair with light brown eyes. He looked pretty tall, or maybe he was just taller than the woman he was standing beside. I assumed she was his wife by the way he had his arm around her waist and their genuine smiles. They looked so happy. I hated to imagine what they looked like now because of the accident.

I laid the report beside me and rubbed my temples. I needed a break. As I shifted in my bed, my papers and pens fell to the floor.

When I reached down and started to pick everything up, my thumb caught on a bright blue string that was under the bed. I unfolded the wrinkled ball of material and was surprised to find that it was my summer league swimsuit.

The last time that I had worn it, I won first place. I sighed as I realized that I would never feel the exhilaration of winning again. Thinking about my team kind of made me miss it but only for a second.

Even if I wanted to try and swim again... I looked out my window that overlooked our untouched pool. Normally during this point in the summer, it was never empty. My friends and I would be outside from sunrise to sunset.

But, no one had been swimming in our pool since the accident. It was really sad, actually. Every morning when I came downstairs, I looked out the big sliding glass doors expecting Liam to be out there already, but it was always desolate. Sometimes I would see him gazing outside, and even though he tried to hide his emotions, he had a look of longing all over his face.

One day when I was coming downstairs for dinner, I heard him crying. He was talking to Mom and Dad about wanting to swim. They told him that it was too complicated and that they were very sorry. It made me feel awful. I hated that I was the reason he wasn't enjoying his summer as much as he should've been.

While staring out my window, my mind was whirring. *Could I try? No. No I couldn't. But... maybe I could? No.* I decided to brush the thought away when someone walked outside and caught my eye.

Liam walked out the sliding doors and sat in one of our lounge chairs. He stared at the lapping water until finally, his emotions melted and he started to cry. Once again, I had forgotten he was so young. His cry, though, reminded me. He became an eight-year-old boy again, devastated that his summer was wasting away without touching the chlorine water.

My heart fell to my feet when I got off my bed, rushed down the stairs, and passed my parents in the kitchen. They were watching him, probably because they had talked to him about swimming again. He didn't notice me until I was sitting down beside him; he looked at me like I was the last person he wanted to see.

Between sobbing breaths, he told me to go away.

"What's wrong?" I asked, even though I already knew the answer. He was frowning and his eyes were red with anger. He rarely ever threw fits anymore and it surprised me.

"You're ruining my summer!"

Ouch. I didn't know how to respond. Technically, I wasn't the person who told him he couldn't swim; my parents were. They didn't even ask me about it. I didn't say anything though because I didn't disagree with their thinking. I was a little worried how it would feel if there were other people swimming around me.

After a long moment of my searching for a response, he stood up. The distressed look that was plastered on his face bothered me. He started to walk to the gate that led to the backyard when I interrupted his anger with my own.

"Liam, you're being ridiculous." He turned towards me with fresh tears.

"You're not letting me swim!"

"You have no idea how hard this is for me. Stop complaining about your horrible summer. At least this isn't happening to you."

He didn't reply. Instead, he shoved the gate open and slammed it behind him.

"Ugh!" I yelled. Then Dad came outside.

"What was that all about?"

"Don't worry. I'll follow him," I said without explaining. When I started walking to the beach, I felt absolutely horrible about yelling at him. I was being so selfish. This was affecting everyone, not just me.

I was absorbed in my own thoughts, until I took the first step in the sand. I slowed to a stop when I realized where I was. I hadn't been to the beach in what felt like years. At least I could tolerate looking at the pool, but it was so hard to look at the ocean. The water was pitch black in the setting sun and impossible to see through. The waves crashed onto the beach, seemingly trying to reach me and trap me again. I almost turned around, but I couldn't leave him without apologizing.

I slowly walked to where he was sitting. He was still staring out into the sea, but I knew he heard me standing there. I noticed he wasn't crying anymore. He probably felt just as bad about us arguing as I did.

"Hey, Liam. I'm sorry," I said with regret, while I struggled to find a way to sit in the sand without getting it all over me.

"You don't have to sit. I'll stand," he offered as he stood up. "There is nothing for you to be sorry about. It's not your fault that you're scared of the water. I would be too if... ya know. I was just being immatrue."

The corners of my lips went up and I held in a laugh. He had pronounced the 'ture' in immature like 'true.' I started to laugh out loud.

"What's so funny?"

"It's imma*ture*, not imma*true*," I replied through a smile.

"Oh. I was being immature."

I looked at my little brother. I felt terrible for him that he and everyone else had been sucked into this mess. Liam was apologizing for wanting to enjoy his summer. He was *eight*. He *should* have been upset.

"Liam."

"Mh hm?"

"You're going to swim."

"Really?"

"And so am I."

CHAPTER 27

I'M SO PROUD OF YOU!

"**E**mmi! This is incredible," Jess said with glee when she read my notebook page. For the whole week, I had only written: I'm swimming tomorrow.

"No, it's really not," I mumbled. I had my elbows on my knees and my fingers on my temples. "Every time I even *think* about swimming I feel sick." I looked up at her and sarcastically said, "So I've been sick for the past five days."

"Well, that explains the bad handwriting and frowning faces scribbled all over the page."

"Why would I *say* that?" I moaned, as I fell backwards on the couch. "I can't swim! My fear of water didn't just magically disappear!"

"Why don't you tell your family that you don't feel ready?"

"I can't. The other day, I gathered them in the kitchen to tell them I couldn't do it. Liam had a feeling I was going to back out. You should've seen his face. So I made up some excuse to move it from Saturday to Sunday."

"But you're swimming tomorrow?"

"Yeah. Then there was an excuse for Sunday and Monday too." I sat up and looked at her with pleading eyes. "What should I do?"

"You should swim."

"I can't."

"Then you shouldn't swim."

"But I can't do that either."

"Emmi, I can't make this decision for you. You showered and drank water. Maybe you're ready to swim. If you're not, I think your family would understand. Liam might be a little disappointed, but like you've said, all he wants is for you to get better." I weighed my options for a few moments and thought about each point she'd made.

"You're right. They'll understand. I'm not ready and I'm not going to force myself to be."

After my session, I was fully prepared to tell everyone that I would not be swimming the next day. But before I walked through the door, I got a text from Liz.

Liz: ur mom told us abt tomorrow. I'm so proud of you! would it be okay if i came?

I decided I would reply after I broke the news to my family. When I kicked off my shoes in the foyer, Mom heard me from the living room.

"Hey, Emmi. How'd your session go?"

"Good," I replied nervously.

Just then, Liam burst through the back door sweating and panting. He ran over and hugged me.

"Ew! Stop! You're disgusting."

"I was playing volleyball with Dad." He walked to the kitchen to get a drink.

"It is hot out there," Dad said as he came in. "I can't wait to cool off in the pool tomorrow."

I flinched.

"Honey, have we told you how proud we are of you?" Mom asked.

"Yes, many times," I grumbled. She didn't hear me.

"We are just so happy that you've decided to take this next step in your recovery. You're *so* brave."

"I can't wait for you to remember how much you love swimming," Dad added.

"Me too," I answered. Then I immediately ran up to my room.

What? Me too? Why did I say that? Why didn't I tell them?

I collapsed on my bed and groaned. I couldn't tell them that I wasn't swimming. They would be so disappointed. So, I pulled out my phone and texted Liz.

Emmi: See u tomorrow

CHAPTER 28

YEAH, SURE. OKAY. WHY DO YOU ASK?

When I came down the stairs, Mom said, "Emmi, I couldn't find your favorite swimsuit."

"That one? Oh, well, it's okay." I tried really hard to hide the fact that I knew where it was: long gone after I threw it away in my hospital room. That felt like years ago.

"I'm just so happy that you're ready to give this a try, honey," Dad said, while applying sunscreen to Liam's forehead.

Psh. Ready? I didn't feel ready whatsoever.

Then I heard the door open. Liz and Elliot walked in. They were smiling, but I wasn't.

"Hey, everyone!" Liz said, as Elliot shut the door behind them. I didn't say anything for a second; I just gave Liz a look. Then I noticed Elliot looking at me too.

"H-hi!" I said and bolted to give Liz a hug. Then I awkwardly waved at Elliot and he awkwardly waved back. When he was distracted by questions from my parents, I pulled Liz into the living room.

"What's he doing here?" I demanded furiously.

"Elliot? Sorry. I assumed you told him you were going to swim, so I asked if he wanted to carpool. When he didn't know what I was talking about, I had to explain it. By then it was too late to take back my offer."

"Why would you assume that I wanted my ex-boyfriend here in the first place?"

Liz began to reply, but Liam's excited yelp interrupted her.

"I didn't get your ears!" Dad yelled, as he grabbed him just before he got outside. He picked him up, lifted him over his shoulder, and tickled him. Liam burst into laughter when Dad threw him on the couch.

"Are you excited to swim, Liam?" Liz asked with enthusiasm.

"Yes! Yes! *Yes!* Dad, hurry up!" he begged, while shoving the sunscreen into Dad's hands.

I realized that I wasn't laughing with everyone else, so I quickly jumped into a nervous laugh. When I accidentally made eye contact with Elliot, I knew he could see the discomfort all over my face. Everyone was looking forward to something that I knew wasn't going to happen.

In a high-pitched voice, I said, "I'm going to go put my hair up." I turned around and took the stairs two at a time to my bedroom.

Before I walked through my door, someone said my name.

"Emmi?" I jumped and whipped around to face him.

"Sorry, I didn't mean to scare you."

"Uh, it's fine." Tears were threatening my eyes. All I wanted to do was lock myself away and never come out. Elliot sensed this.

"Emmi, are you doing okay?"

"Yeah, sure. Okay. Why do you ask?"

"You said you had to put up your hair, but it already is."

I reached up, only to find that it was in a perfect ponytail.

"I wanted to fix it," I said, making a poor effort to cover up my poor excuse. As I dropped my hand, I tried to pull out a couple strands without him noticing. It was just my luck; my fingers got caught and I had to stop and untangle them from my hair.

Thankfully, he ignored my mistake. "Look, I'm sorry I came. At first I was angry that you didn't tell me. I guess I thought I was a part of this now."

Rage pulsated through me. He was *angry with me?* Just because he was my last resort ride home didn't mean everything was normal between us. We hadn't talked since the hospital because I had been ignoring his texts and calls. I just didn't know where we stood anymore. We had agreed to be friends, but I didn't know if that was possible.

"Then I realized that it didn't matter how I felt, Emmi. I just wanted to be here to support you. I can go if my being here makes you uncomfortable."

And that was why I dated Elliot for three years.

I finally looked right into his eyes and butterflies flooded my stomach.

Just then, as I opened my mouth, we heard people yelling from outside.

"Oh! Liam!"

CHAPTER 29

SEE? YOU WERE OVERREACTING

L iam puked into the pool. He had been so excited that he was running in circles, jumping up and down and laughing hysterically. As soon as he stood on the edge ready to cannonball, the huge leftover breakfast he'd had landed in the water.

Even though he said his stomach felt better, he was more concerned that he and I had to wait even longer to swim. Mom still made him lie down for a while, where he threw a fit and cried until he fell asleep.

Elliot, Liz, and I stood in the kitchen eating chips, talking, and pretending to feel bad for Liam. We all did, of course, but he would get over it.

My friends and parents were mostly worried about me and my confidence. I could tell by the way that Elliot kept scratching his head, how Liz kept giving me half-hugs, how Mom kept staring at me with sympathy, and how Dad kept looking down at his feet.

Little did they know that I didn't have any confidence to begin with.

Without a word, Dad walked out the sliding glass doors. I decided to follow him to break the tension in the house.

He was searching the storage closet, which made me curious. "What are you looking for?"

"Well, it turns out we ran out of chlorine for the pool. Just in time," he replied sarcastically without turning around. His voice was strained with the longing for me to get better. "I'll have to run uptown before we can do anything else." He desperately continued to rummage through the closet.

"I'll pick it up, Dad. I'll get in and out, so that we can clean the pool as fast as possible."

"Really? Thanks, honey. I can start making dinner."

"Make mac-and-cheese. That'll cheer Liam up." It was mostly an excuse to have something other than spaghetti for dinner, but I didn't tell him that.

Dad wasn't super good at being an emotional support, so cooking, making us laugh, and taking care of the house were things he did to make us feel better. Don't get me wrong; he understood us. He was just kind of awkward when it came to handling sadness. He didn't like seeing the people he loved in pain.

"Thanks again, honey."

I walked quickly to my car, instead of going through the house. When I got to the front door, I stuck my head in and snatched the keys that were sitting in a bowl on the small table in the foyer. I grabbed them as fast as I could before anyone could see me. I was trying to avoid Liz's offers to come with me.

When I got to my car, I slammed the door behind me and started the engine. As I pulled out, I took deep breaths in and deep breaths out.

"You got out of it today," I said to myself, "but you have to tell them you're not ready."

My fears and worries surfaced as I drove. I didn't bother to put on the radio, so I sat in silence. The hum of the car was the only noise, along with my swimming thoughts.

I can't tell them now. I'll just have to swim. What if I forget how to? I definitely will. I'm going to drown if I try. I definitely shouldn't risk it. What? I couldn't forget how to swim. I've never gone a day in my life when I didn't know how to swim. It's just not possible. But... it was so terrifying under the boat. I guess I'll just have to avoid swimming for the rest of my life. Wait... I can't do that; I live in Florida. I guess I'm moving. Should I go to Arizona or Ohio?

My random thoughts were interrupted by the sounds of honking vehicles. I blinked and warm tears fell down my face. I sniffled, wiped them with my wrist, and turned to look in the rearview mirror. There were around ten cars lined up behind me, and every driver was honking because I'd been sitting at the same stop sign for far too long.

"Gah!" I choked out. Embarrassment settled in on top of the stress. When I pulled into the parking lot at Clark's, I calmed down.

We had large chain grocery stores on Captiva Island, but the people who had lived here long enough knew that Clark's was better. He treated everyone like family. I got out of my car and walked to the front doors that opened automatically.

Because the accident had happened approximately two months ago, my face no longer appeared in the local newspaper. Everyone had already read about me online. Mom's phone had stopped blowing up with the same comments on her Facebook page: *Praying for you and your family... Get well soon Emmi... I'm here for you, Bethany.* Kids from my school stopped staring at me or tapping me on the back to ask how I was doing. Everyone knew my story now and treated me like a normal person. The problem was, they probably thought I was fully recovered and swimming again. I didn't try to correct them.

"Hi, Emmi! Haven't seen you in a while. How are you doing?" Clark asked.

"I'm doing fine. I'm just picking up some chlorine for the pool." I wasn't really in the mood for small talk; I just wanted to get back to my car.

I walked to the back of the store towards the pool supplies. On my way, I passed a man who was organizing the shelves of sunscreen and pool toys.

"Hello," I said absentmindedly as I walked past him.

"Hello, how are y-" he started to say from behind me. The noise of the shuffling boxes suddenly stopped and the man was silent. He didn't finish his sentence. As I turned the corner of the aisle, I caught a glimpse of him. He was staring right at me. His eyes followed me around the corner, but the rest of him didn't. A chill ran down my spine. *What in the world?*

I kept walking and pretended that I was looking around. I still hadn't heard any movement from him and it freaked me out. *Did I say something?* Then his footsteps started to walk towards me, very fast. I panicked and started to speed walk to the next aisle before he could see me. But he kept following me. *What's happening?*

Suddenly, a box fell behind me. I flinched and started to walk even faster. *No, no, no.* I turned the next corner and so did he. *Please no.* We were getting to the end of the rows of aisles. *Go away, go away.* When I ducked behind a candy display, he saw me immediately. I stood up and ran back to the pool aisle. *No, no, no, no, no!*

I skidded to a stop when I reached the same sunscreen shelf that the man had been organizing only minutes ago. I stood like a statue and listened but didn't hear more footsteps. I let out a sigh of relief. *See? You were overreacting.* When I caught my breath, I resumed looking for the chlorine.

When I finished shopping, I walked to the cash register. I counted to make sure I had enough sticks of chlorine in my arms before sprawling them on the counter.

"Whew! I totally thought I was going to drop these."

When I looked up, Clark was looking at me with pity. My heart sank when I realized the man who I thought had been chasing me was standing right next to him.

His arms were down at his sides and his mouth was agape. He had dark brown, unbrushed graying hair. He had light brown, stressed, sleep-deprived eyes. He was very tall and familiar looking...

I shuddered. I had never met this man before, yet I knew every detail of his life. We had never crossed paths, but instead, we were hurtled into each other, sending both of our lives in a spiraling crash.

My voice could barely speak his name.

"Captain Benny?"

CHAPTER 30

I'M TRULY, INCREDIBLY SORRY

I tried not to cringe when he asked if we could talk. *You have to do this, Emmi, for your own sake.* I reluctantly agreed to discuss everything that had happened since the accident over food. Even though I knew it would be hard, I had to hear the truth.

I was trembling when the waiter brought our orders.

"Mm, this is great," he said with a mouthful of fish.

"Cool," I said uncomfortably. "So, Cap- Mr. Benny, how are you?"

He swallowed and put down his fork. He folded his hands on the table, then unfolded them, then folded them again. "To be honest... I'm not great. No, not great at all." He unfolded his hands again. "I'm sorry for scaring you earlier. I was nervous, too, when I saw you. We were both caught off guard. I just wasn't thinking."

"It's alright." There was a deafening silence before he spoke.

"Emmi, how are you doing?"

"Well, I-" I cleared my throat, "um, better."

"Better? Your ankle?"

At first I was confused, but then I realized that he didn't know the extent of the toll that the accident had on me. "Oh! My ankle? It's long healed. So are my muscles and bruises; my lungs are strong again."

"Well then, why just 'better'? Why not great?"

"You know, the accident did more than damage me physically. It's affected me emotionally," I stammered. "I haven't, uh, actually swum since... since it happened."

He stared at me in disbelief. "What? I had no idea." He ran his hands through his hair and looked at me in anguish. "This is all my fault."

"Mr. Benny-"

"I can't believe this. It was bad enough knowing I almost killed you. I ruined your life," he interrupted in a slightly raised voice.

"What?" I said, taken aback.

"You were the captain of the swim team throughout high school, and you have some sort of record for holding your breath underwater. All you *do* is swim. It's your whole life, and I've ruined it. Why do I always ruin everything? I can't do one thing right," he answered with regret.

Just then, I stood up so fast that I didn't realize I was doing it.

"Mr. Benny, it may seem like you've taken everything away from me, but you *can not* tell me that my life is ruined. Yes, swimming was a major part of it. In fact, it was everything to me, and it still may be one day. But it wasn't my entire life. I'm only eighteen. My life can't be ruined; I haven't even started college! You may have done research on me or whatever, but there is more to me than you think. And stop blaming yourself. It happened. There's nothing we can do to change it. I didn't have to be the only person on the deck at that moment, but I was."

I finished talking and gingerly sat back down. He was looking at me with sorrow. He paused for a moment and took in my entire speech. "Emmi, I'm truly, incredibly sorry. I didn't mean to assume that."

I nodded my head and checked the time on my phone. It was almost six. I needed to hurry this up.

"Mr. Benny, why did you fall asleep?" I asked boldly. He gave me a look that showed I had crossed an unspoken line.

"Emmi..."

"If you want to make everything better, I need answers."

Our eyes locked, and a sense of understanding passed through us. We used to be two normal people, but now we were broken. We were so sick and tired of having the effects of this crash weighing on every aspect of our lives. We both knew that we needed each other to make things a little easier. He just needed to answer my question.

"You know the picture they gave you in my profile, of my-" he corrected himself, "that woman and me? Well, things have changed. Her name is Angelina. She was my high school sweetheart; she was the most beautiful, kind, smart and funny girl I ever knew. My wife was the woman of my dreams. We were married for twenty-one years. *Twenty-one.* Anyway, about a year ago, I lost my job as a lawyer. That job was paying for everything in our lives. Because I was fired, it was impossible to find work."

He took a drink of water and continued. "Angelina and I started to argue over my finding another job. Then we started to have trouble with money, which caused even more fighting and stress. She had to start working double shifts at the general store and we barely crossed paths. Whenever we did, we were too angry or tired to have a conversation. Then one day she sat me down to talk."

Tears filled his eyes. "She... she wanted a divorce." As soon as he spoke, I felt his pain.

"She told me that the love between us had faded and that she was tired of being angry all the time. I tried to tell her that we could work it out, but she said it was too late; she'd made up her mind long ago. I wanted to make her happy, so I agreed to let her go."

"I let the love of my life go."

Then, after a moment, he sat up straighter and wiped his eyes. "The day that the boat crashed was the day that I was supposed to go to the house one last time to pack the rest of my belongings and leave her forever. It would be the last time that I would look at her face and see in her eyes the pain *I'd* caused. Because I was terrified of this, I decided instead to fill in for my friend, Captain Tracey, when he was going to be on vacation. By the way, he sued me as soon as he learned that I crashed his boat."

"Some friend," I interrupted.

"It really just made the situation even worse. Anyway, I thought taking the shift would distract me from the worst day of my life. But, as you can imagine, I didn't sleep a wink the night before. I reflected on the life I was going to be leaving behind the next day. Every. Single. Memory. I wished and prayed to go back to even the little moments when we were happy. The next thing I knew, it was time to wake up. I was so tired that morning that I can't even remember getting on the boat. Anyway, you know the rest of the story."

When he finished, there was a pang in my heart that I hoped nobody would ever have to feel for someone. When I got up, so did he. We hugged and cried and sympathized with each other. Once the tears began to ease, we let go and looked at each other.

"Emmi, even though I don't know the whole you, I know you are going to get through this. Don't give up."

I smiled. "Mr. Benny, you deserve to be just as happy as Angelina. You are not allowed to give up either. Things will turn around; I know it."

"Thank you for meeting me and I hope I will be able to talk to you again. I need to go home now."

We said our goodbyes and on our way out the door, I paused and said, "Mr. Benny?"

"Yes?"

"I accept your apology. I don't blame you for what happened to me. Not at all."

CHAPTER 31

HE'S NOT IMPORTANT

"So, what are we talking about today?" Jess asked when I handed her my notebook. She read it silently, then addressed the first thing on the list. "Not pressing charges? On Captain Benny, you mean?"

"Yes." Then I told her how I ran into him and learned the story of Angelina. Jess's eyebrows went up and down and she occasionally gasped.

"That's crazy!"

"I know. I mailed the legal papers yesterday."

"Why did that story help you to not press charges?"

"Because all he did was love someone. And I know, drowsy driving is a problem, but he didn't deserve any more challenges." I thought of his tired eyes and sober face. "I could tell everything was already weighing on him enough."

"That's so kind, Emmi. I definitely wouldn't have done that myself," she laughed. "Tell me why in the next line you've written that you're not swimming."

"Oh, yeah. You know how I said that I couldn't disappoint everyone, and how Liam threw up in the pool? Well, I kind of took that as another opportunity to tell my family how I was feeling. After I filled out Captain Benny's papers, I told them I wasn't swimming. You were right. My parents felt terrible for adding pressure and said that I could take my time. Liam cried, but he told me later that it was okay."

"That's great. You are so lucky to have your family." She looked back at the last thing I had written.

"That's it. I'll take that back now," I said, as I jerked out my hand.

"Hold on. Who's Elliot?"

"No one. Can I have the notebook?"

"Emmi, tell me who Elliot is."

"Does it say Elliot? I meant to write Elizabeth."

She crossed her arms and raised an eyebrow. "Okay then. What happened with Liz this week?"

"Um, she…" I hesitated for too long. Jess knew I was lying.

"Emiline, I thought we agreed to communicate."

"I am!"

"Then why are you lying about Elliot?"

"He's not important. I shouldn't have written his name down." She paused and put her hand on her chin. She squinted at me and nodded.

"Elliot is your boyfriend."

"No, he's not."

"He's not your boyfriend *anymore*."

I glared at her. "I'm supposed to be seeing a therapist, not a mind-reader."

"Ha ha!" she laughed in accomplishment. "They are one in the same." I continued to frown at her. "Why haven't you told me about him before?"

I sank on the couch and started to mess with the edge of a pillow. "Because I don't really know what he is to me anymore."

"Can you explain your relationship and how you broke up?"

So, I explained everything. I told her about us when we were kids, how we got to know each other, when we started dating, and how smoothly things went through the years. Then I told her how our relationship started to fade, until we broke up. I also told her that I friendzoned him, that he convinced me to go to therapy, and that he supported me when I was afraid to swim again. It felt strange to express my feelings about my relationship with him. I hadn't really done that with anyone since the crash.

When I finished, the first thing Jess had to say was, "Well, hats off to Elliot for getting you here."

I didn't laugh.

She dropped her smile and continued. "Your relationship seems very messy right now. And I agree that you didn't necessarily treat him the best when you were dating. But you can't keep ignoring this obviously unsolved break-up forever. You need to tell him how you feel, no matter how confused you are. Everyone involved in this accident has matured in some way this summer. Who knows? Maybe you and Elliot are ready to give it another chance."

Then she handed me the notebook. "From what you've told me, Elliot loved you very much."

I pulled my hand away and the notebook smacked the floor. "No, he didn't," I said with horror on my face.

She looked at me in shock. "What do you mean? Of course he did! And it sounds like he still does."

I only replied, "No."

She gazed at me for a moment and once again, read my mind. "You never told him that you loved him?"

I shook my head.

"Why not?"

"I don't know... He just never said it, so I didn't either."

Neither of us said another word for minutes.

Finally, Jess leaned forward and asked, "What if he wanted you to say it first?"

CHAPTER 32

I ALREADY TOLD YOU

No matter how hard I tried, I couldn't get Jess's words out of my mind. What if she was right? What if Elliot wanted me to say it first? But it was Elliot. He was the most romantic person I'd ever met. If he loved me, he would've said it.

Even if I tried to convince myself Jess was wrong, every time I saw Elliot after that session, a war started in my head. Whenever we were with Liz, I would momentarily zone out staring at him, trying to find any signs he might be sending me. But then he would notice me looking at him and it would get weird.

One day, Liz had asked me and Elliot if we wanted to hang out. We were sitting in her living room when the show we were watching went to a commercial.

"Bathroom break!" Liz said when she jumped up. I quickly picked up my phone and pretended to text someone.

"Hey, Emmi."

"Huh?" I replied, not looking up from my phone.

"Do you love me?" I raised my eyebrows and I immediately stood up.

"What did you just say?" I demanded.

Elliot narrowed his eyes and offered me the bowl of popcorn. "I asked if you are hungry."

I breathed a heavy sigh of relief and sat back down. "No thanks." Even when I turned back to my phone, I could still feel his gaze on me.

"So, Emmi," Liz began when she came back into the room, "Elliot and I have something we want to ask you."

"Okay," I replied slowly.

"We don't expect you to do it," Elliot said quickly, "if you don't want to."

"Do what?"

"Do you remember that you volunteered to have the summer party with our graduating class?" she asked.

I tipped my head back and admitted, "I completely forgot."

At the end of our senior year, the student council decided that we should have a party during the summer where everyone in our class was invited. We would get together to have one last high school party before heading off to college. I volunteered my house, and everyone agreed it was the perfect place.

Now when I thought about seventy-ish people at my house splashing water everywhere, running around, probably breaking things, yelling, and blasting music, it made me feel sick to my stomach. The party would be two weeks from then, so it didn't leave me much time. Although, I really wanted to see my friends and pretend everything was normal for once. I wanted to be reminded of how everything used to be.

"Yeah, I don't know... I'm not sure if I'm ready."

"Everyone knows what happened to you. They'll probably be extra careful," Elliot reassured me.

"Well, I won't swim at my own pool party. Isn't that weird?"

"What are you talking about? Only half of the people who go to pool parties *actually* end up swimming. I won't swim either. We can start up a beach volleyball team," Liz answered.

It sounded to me like they were looking forward to it. Even though they acted like they would understand if I wasn't ready, I could tell they, and everyone else, would be disappointed.

"Alright, I'll do it. As long as you three help organize it." They cheered and high-fived; then Liz tilted her head.

"What do you mean *three*?" she asked.

"You two, me, and Nelly," I replied cautiously.

Liz looked me right in the eyes. "Emmi, I already told you…"

Then I noticed Elliot's nervous expression and guilty eyes.

"Are you kidding me? You know too?" I snipped.

"Please don't bring me into this," he begged.

"If whatever happened to Nelly is so bad, why does he know? My *ex-boyfriend* gets to see her, but not me?" I shouted at Liz.

"Are you being serious right now?" Elliot said with disgust. I was so shocked by his outburst that I didn't answer. So, he stood up and promptly left the house.

I followed him.

CHAPTER 33

TELL HIM HOW YOU FEEL

"**E**lliot!" I called, while running out the front door. He was sitting in his car about to drive away. When he noticed me, he rolled his eyes and got out.

"I'm surprised you followed me," he said with anger. I stopped when I reached him and furrowed my brow.

"What's that supposed to mean?"

"*Please* don't act like you're the victim right now." I opened my mouth, but he interrupted. "Stop! I've never in our three-year relationship *ever* yelled at you. I think the first time I even stood up for myself was when we broke up. I'm sorry, Emmi, but I'm *done* falling at your feet when you don't even have the decency to give me a little respect."

"Where is this coming from?" I asked, baffled.

"Just now! Yes, we are broken up. Therefore ex-boyfriend would technically be something that I am. But, Emmi, *it's us!* You're acting like I'm some guy you dated for a month. We agreed to be friends, so I am giving my absolute best effort to be just that. But you're completely ignoring me! I can't *bring* myself to call you my ex-girlfriend. I probably never will. You mean so much more to me than that. I guess I thought you felt the same way when you said I deserved better than you."

"Elliot, I'm so sorry," I whispered.

"No. How am I supposed to believe you? Your words don't mean anything anymore. Actually, they haven't for a long time."

"I know," I cried. "I'm *so* sorry."

"I tried so hard for you. While we were dating and after. But let's admit it. You've never cared about me as much as I do about you. You stopped trying a long time ago. And I know, I *know* things are *so* hard right now. But I just can't do this anymore." He opened his car and started to get in.

"Elliot, please don't go," I sobbed.

"Emmi, I'm sorry. I can't handle it anymore." He looked at me with tears rolling down his cheeks. "This, us. It's drowning me." He got into his car and slammed the door.

"Wait," I said in panic. He was really leaving. He was really giving up. He started the car.

"Stop! Can we please talk?" I put my hands on my head as the image of his smiling face started to fade. I couldn't lose him. I just couldn't bear it.

Time seemed to stop and I was transported back under that ship. I'd thought I was never going to see him again. I'd thought I would never get the chance to make things right. But when I was given a second chance, I still didn't. I couldn't let myself push him away again. I was reminded of Jess's words. *Elliot loved you very much. Maybe you and Elliot are ready to give it another chance. What if he wanted you to say it first?*

Tell him how you feel.

So, I did.

"I love you! Elliot Peters, I *love* you!"

He paused with his hand on the gear. He stared ahead and took a deep breath. Finally, he met my eyes through the windshield.

Then he drove away.

CHAPTER 34

WE ALL HAVE OUR STORIES

"Emmi, can you tell me what's wrong?" Jess asked. That Monday, I had walked into her office without saying anything. I just sat on my couch, pulled my knees to my chest, and stared at the floor.

I didn't feel like talking. I hadn't since I told Elliot I loved him. First of all, I didn't think I would be able to explain how he felt about me without choking up. I had really never experienced heartbreak before, and it was agony. Even though I shouldn't have been, I was embarrassed. I knew everything he had said was true, and I didn't want to admit that to anyone yet. So, I hadn't told anyone about the fight for a week.

"You're scaring me…" Jess said.

"I'm okay," I replied so quietly that it was nearly inaudible.

"No, you're not. You haven't acted like this since your first session. What happened?"

"Jess, how did you know you loved Jeremy?"

"Um," she said, taken aback. "What?"

"How did you know you loved your fiancé?"

"Let's not talk about me."

"Please?" I pleaded. I looked up at her. I saw the realization cross her face, as she understood why I was asking.

"Well, it's a pretty long story. It's also *not* a fairy tale, like you might imagine. Promise me you'll tell me what's bothering you when I finish?"

I hesitated but nodded.

"When I was in high school, there was this guy I was dating. Unlike your relationship, mine was a more laid-back type. At least that's what I thought. This boy was a good-looking teenage jock. I never thought we actually had any connection; I just wanted to have fun in high school. When the end of my senior year came around, I tried to end things before we moved on to different colleges. But he didn't like that. We got into a huge fight, and it ended with him hitting me."

"No," I said in shock.

She swallowed and nodded her head. "He apologized over and over, and I made the mistake of forgiving him out of fear. So, we started college as a couple. The first weekend, he came to visit without telling me. I didn't really want to see him, so I got angry. Again, we fought and it ended with him hitting me. But that time, he didn't apologize. He pretended like nothing happened and stayed the rest of the weekend."

Jess took a deep breath and continued. "I remember being scared when the weeks ended. Every Friday at seven, he would arrive and I wouldn't see any of my friends. He never wanted to meet anyone or even leave my dorm room. As time went on, the abuse became more apparent and intense. I always had new bruises every Monday when I went back to class. People kept asking me if everything was okay, but I never told them what was happening. I eventually pushed everyone else away but him."

Tears started to form in my eyes, but I willed myself not to cry.

"One day, towards the end of my freshman year, we got into a small disagreement. He resorted to his regular ways and smacked me. That time, instead of cowering, I hit him back. Before I knew it, I was telling him how much I hated him. I screamed everything I had ever felt each time that he had abused me. Let's just say he wasn't happy about it. The next thing I knew, I woke up in a hospital with a broken arm."

I couldn't take it anymore. I covered my eyes, as the tears rolled down my cheeks.

"Emmi, I'm okay," she said, as she moved over and sat next to me. She put her arm around my shoulders and said, "I'll tell you the good part now. When I went home for the summer, I told my family everything. Even though they tried to make me feel better, it didn't help. I didn't leave the house the whole time I was home."

"Then, it was finally time to go back to college. I spent the first semester either at class or in my dorm. I didn't try to make new friends and I definitely stayed away from boys. Instead of going home, I decided to stay at college over Christmas break. One day I was returning some books in the library when a boy asked me what I liked to read."

Jess laughed at the memory. "I kid you not. I was so shy that I didn't even look at him. I tried to walk away, but he kept asking me question after question. When I said I had to go, he asked me to lunch. I said no, but he was persistent. I finally agreed. He gave me his number and his name. Then he left."

"That lunch with Jeremy turned into many more. Before I knew it, I was with him almost every second of every day. When he asked me to be his girlfriend, I was hesitant. He asked me why, and I decided to tell him my story." Jess paused and took a deep breath. "He hugged me for a long time. He promised to never hurt me in any way. He promised to always be patient with me and listen to me. He promised to never leave me. And he kept those promises. He made me feel so safe and supported. He made me feel like a person again. That was when I knew I loved him, and I haven't questioned it since."

"Wow, I had no idea…"

"We all have our stories. That was why I decided to become a therapist. I want to help people like Jeremy helped me." Then she stood up. "Okay, enough about me. Can you tell me what happened?"

"Well, after that, I feel dramatic," I said sarcastically.

"Emmi…"

"Fine."

So, I told her everything. I told her how I said something I shouldn't have. I told her how Elliot completely exploded. I told her how he said he couldn't handle the weight of our relationship anymore. I told her how I'd hurt him more than I realised. I told her how I said I loved him, and I told her how he'd driven away.

"Oh, no," she said, moving back over to my couch.

"You're the first person I've told," I said and wiped my cheeks. "I'm so stupid. He told me he wanted me out of his life and I told him I loved him. Of *course*, he didn't say it back. I just made it worse."

"Well, do you actually love him?"

I paused and thought about how Jess knew she loved Jeremy. He made her feel safe, supported, and loved when no one else could.

"Yes… I think I do."

"I know you're not going to want to hear this, but I didn't want you to tell Elliot how you felt, so that you could get back together. I wanted you to tell him how you felt, so that you would know where you two stood. And although you don't like the answer, you had to know."

A new wave of sadness crashed over me. I touched my neck where my heart necklace used to be. It suddenly felt bare. It felt like the necklace was supposed to be there.

"Look at me," she said. I turned my tear-filled eyes towards her. "If you *really* love him, you will respect his feelings. That is what he's wanted you to do all along, so prove to him that you can. If it's meant to be, he will come back to you. I promise."

I nodded, even though I didn't want to. I knew then more than ever that I wanted to be with Elliot for the rest of my life. I couldn't imagine my future without him. But Jess was right. He had said that I didn't respect him, so that was what I needed to do.

"There's one more thing I wanted to talk about that you mentioned in your story," Jess said.

"What?" I asked, even though I already knew what she was going to say.

"I think you have one more relationship you need to sort out. Let's talk about Nelly."

CHAPTER 35

LIKE I'D JUST MISTAKEN A STRANGER FOR MY BEST FRIEND

While I was sitting at the stoplight, Nelly's house was in view. My heart was beating faster than ever and I was shaking profusely. I tried to tell myself I was just excited to see her, but truthfully, I was so scared.

Jess had suggested that I talk to her in person. I had thought about it before, but I was worried it might be invasive or make things even worse. But, Jess said it had been long enough and that it was the right time.

The light turned green and I started to drive. My knuckles were white around the steering wheel and my back started to sweat. As soon as I pulled into her driveway, I could see her car. She was definitely home.

No excuses now.

Normally, I would've jumped out of my car and walked up to her house like it was my own. I would have walked through her front door without knocking, said hello to her parents, and headed to her bedroom, where she and Liz would have immediately asked me my opinion about a pointless argument they were having.

But things were far from normal. I turned off my car and stared at the house. Possibilities about what she was going to tell me started spinning in my head. *Maybe she is still mad about the fight we had before the accident. Maybe she doesn't want to be my friend anymore. Maybe she's moving. Maybe she's sick. Maybe it's something so bad I can't even see it coming.*

I stepped out of the car and slammed the door behind me. I walked up to her door with a purpose but stopped as soon as I reached my destination. *Knock or doorbell?* I held my fist over the wood, but then hit the doorbell. I had never even noticed that they had a doorbell before. My heart jumped when I heard footsteps coming towards the door. And then it opened.

It was Nelly.

She was wearing, to no surprise, a t-shirt and Nike shorts, and her hair was in a ponytail. Her house seemed normal with quiet, beachy music playing in the background. Her face showed no signs of tears or stress, and she had a smile on her lips. So what was wrong?

My question was answered, as her smile disappeared when she locked eyes with me.

"Nelly!" I exclaimed as I saw her. I wrapped her up in a hug, but she just patted my back.

"Hey, Emiline," she said unenthusiastically. *Emiline? She never calls me Emiline.* I was so nervous that I concocted even more ideas as to why she was ignoring me. *Did I say something wrong in the hospital? Did I forget her birthday? No. Her birthday is in November. Does she think I'm annoying? Does she just really hate me all of a sudden?* I felt my forehead start to sweat.

"Where have you been? I haven't seen you all summer," I asked. She looked at me like she didn't know me. Like she didn't *want* to know me. Like I'd just mistaken a stranger for my best friend.

"Oh, ya know…" she started. Then she just stopped talking and looked everywhere but at me. I'd had enough of her absence.

"No, I don't," I said, heating up quickly. "I was in the hospital, Nelly. Why did you just disappear?"

She stopped pretending to be happy. Even though she glared at me to show that I had taken it a little too far and a little too fast, she stayed silent.

"Do you understand how much I needed and still need you? In case you didn't know, I've been afraid to swim the entire summer."

I threw my hands up. "*Me. Emiline Ganson* is afraid to swim! My life has completely changed and is never going to be the same again. What are you doing that is *so* important that you can't be here for me?"

"I'm sorry this is happening to you," she said promptly, "but I don't want to talk about this right now."

"When will you then, *Penelope?* You've had plenty of time to expl-"

"I said I don't want to talk about this right now," she interrupted. I knew she was not as soft as Liz, but given the circumstances, I thought she would be a little more understanding.

"I'll come to the stupid party Liz told me about. Maybe we can talk then. I don't know. But please leave. I'm not ready."

And just like that, I was looking at the door again.

"Fine!" I screamed, as I trudged to my car. When I started driving, tears of frustration and anger streamed

down my face. Why didn't she want to see me? Why? What
had I done?

"*Not ready? She's* not ready? She's not the one who almost died!" I said to myself. "She told me to leave! I haven't
seen her in months and she told me to leave! What is wrong
with her? Oh wait, she's *not ready.*"

I didn't care if she went to the party. I didn't care if I
ever saw her again. That was her plan all along anyway.

Instead of going home, I drove to Liz's house. As soon
as she opened the door, we hugged. I cried on her shoulder
for reasons she knew, without me having to explain.

I tried to tell myself I was angry because Nelly only
cared about herself, but I knew the real reason was because
I missed her with all my heart.

CHAPTER 36

YOU RUINED EVERYTHING

Another week went by quickly and suddenly, it was the day of the party. Liz and I had made up, but Elliot and I still hadn't talked. Liz never told me whether or not he was still helping with the party; he just never did. So, instead of originally thinking four people were going to plan this, it came down to two.

When I told Jess about my visit to Nelly's house, she said that all I could do now was wait to see if she came. I didn't necessarily like that plan. It just felt so strange to plan a party, while everything around me was crumbling apart.

While Liz was setting out snacks and I was cleaning the living room, I grunted as I pulled yet another candy wrapper from between the couch cushions. "Does Liam think the couch is a trash can or something?" Liz didn't answer. Another moment passed when I started to look under the couch. "No wonder he has no matching socks; they're all under here!" I yelled.

"Emmi, calm down."

"I'm calm." Then I looked back under the couch. "Where did this stain come from?"

"Emmi," Liz said, as she walked over and grabbed my hand. "Are you alright?"

"Nelly won't come. I know it." I pouted, as I tried to hold back tears.

"You don't know that. She said she would be here."

"You should've heard her. She sounded like I was the last person she wanted to see."

"You need to stop thinking about her," Liz advised.

"That's easy for you to say." I let go of her hand. "She's talked to you, she's seen you, and you know the reason she doesn't want to see me. I don't feel in the party mood. I'm going to go sit for a minute." I set my handful of candy wrappers and socks on the ottoman and stepped outside.

I walked past the pool, through the gate, through our backyard, and down the sandy path that led right to the beach.

I used to love nights like this. The weather was perfect. I was all by myself and that was okay. Before the accident, I would bring my favorite beach towel and either read, unwind on my phone, finish my homework, or just watch the beautiful sunset. I would often think how lucky I was to be living in such paradise.

Now, I sat as far away from the water as I could. I watched the waves with resentment, pondering how much had changed in so little time.

I couldn't stop thinking how different my life would've been if I hadn't gone through the accident. I would've been worried about normal things like college. Instead, I was worried about how to avoid water at all costs.

I was starting to second guess what I told Mr. Benny about my life not being over. Of course I survived, and I was grateful for that, but swimming *was* my life. At least he could get on with his because I didn't press any charges.

I dug my fist into the sand and threw it as hard as I could at the ocean.

"You ruined everything!" I yelled at the waves. I cried and screamed and pounded the sand. I didn't care who saw or heard me. "Nothing is ever going to get better and it's all your fault!"

I cried until I couldn't breathe, a feeling that I knew all too well.

CHAPTER 37

THE EMMI THAT ALMOST DROWNED

"**G**et it, Emmi!" someone yelled. I was daydreaming too much and missed the bump.

"No!" Liz said, as she put her hands on her head.

The party was in full swing, and so far everyone was enjoying it but me. Liz and I were playing beach volleyball against two boys from our class, Will and Justin. We had lost three games in a row, thanks to my lack of concentration.

"Yes!" the guys yelled as they high-fived.

"We're getting you back," Liz joked, as she pointed two fingers from her eyes to them.

"So you guys want to play another game?" Justin asked with a smirk.

"In a bit. I'm going to go check on everyone."

I walked back to the pool and looked around. My class-mates were throwing a football in the pool, chatting in the hot tub, sitting by the fire, and dancing to the loud music. Everyone I passed said hi to me, but none of them were Nelly. It was seven thirty-two; the party had been going on for an hour and a half. She wasn't there and I doubted if she was ever going to be.

I passed the pool and tried to stay calm when splashing water came dangerously close to me. My fear of water had been tugging at me the entire night. *What if I panic? I can't swim! What if I don't remember how? Why is everyone looking at me? Are they making fun of me for not swimming at my own pool party?*

"Emmi?"

I was startled when I heard my name. I looked back at the clock. Seven thirty-six. I had been staring at the pool for almost four minutes when I finally acknowledged the person standing beside me.

"Emmi?" the voice asked again. I turned and saw Liz. Her brow was wrinkled with worry and her eyes were curious.

"Sorry, what did you ask?" I said, trying to act normal.

"Emmi, you're acting weird," she said with concern. "Are you okay?"

"I'm fine," I replied quickly.

No I wasn't. The whole night I had been staring at the entrance to the backyard, waiting for Nelly to walk through. Waiting for her to finally tell me what was going on. Waiting for her to just be my friend again. But she never came, and it was distracting me.

"You don't seem fine," she said, as she put her hands on my shoulders.

Just then, a boy wearing a hat and holding an empty container walked over to us. "A few of us are fishing on the beach and we ran out of bait. Do you have more?"

"Um," I said, thinking back to when we set out supplies for fishing. I remembered that Mom hadn't bought enough bait. I decided that if they ran out, I would just tell them to do something else. But when he asked for more, it turned out to be my perfect escape. "No, we don't have any left. I can run to the marina and get more."

"Oh, no, you don't have to do that," he replied instantly.

"It's okay. It'll only take a few minutes," I insisted.

"And I'll drive," Liz interjected. I opened my mouth to stop her, but her expression made it clear that I wasn't going alone.

"Okay. If you really want to," he answered sheepishly.

"Keep an eye on everything while we're gone," Liz said. He nodded and we got in her car.

"Why do you need to go all the way to the marina to get bait? I'm sure they could've found something else to do."

"I just need to get away for a bit," I answered, while looking out the window.

"Emmi," Liz began, as she let out a sigh. "I didn't want to tell you this because I didn't want it to ruin your night, but it seems like you're doing that yourself."

"What?" I grunted, as I turned to her.

"Nelly texted me right before the party started. She's not coming."

I turned back to the window. I wasn't surprised. I was just continually disappointed. If demanding her to talk to me wasn't the solution, I didn't know what was. I was starting to think I would never see her again.

When Liz pulled into the marina, I realized that I hadn't really thought this through.

"Uh..." Liz said, with a look of urgency. "I'll go get the bait. Do you want to stay here?"

I looked around at the boat-filled dock. A million memories from the worst day of my life flooded back. I could still recall every second of the morning leading up to the accident, and I seemed to be watching it again like a movie that I'd already seen.

All of the progress I'd made and every step that I'd taken towards recovery seemed to vanish. I was no longer the Emmi that could shower, drink water, be around swimmers, or even think about water.

I was the Emmi that almost drowned.

I closed my eyes and sank in my seat. "Emmi? Let's just go home. I'm so *stupid*," she mumbled, as she put the car in reverse.

I opened my eyes and looked back at the dock. As people stepped on and off their boats, I wanted to jump out of the car and scream at them to stop. To get away from those monstrous ships while they could. I looked at the fishermen and saw how close they were to the water. I wanted to tell them how that seemingly calm ocean had almost ended my life.

As I looked farther, I noticed someone fishing at the end of the dock. I squinted at the familiar figure. When he turned his head, I knew.

"Liz, stop the car!"

"What?"

"You go get the bait. I'll be right back."

CHAPTER 38

I KNOW FOR SURE

Somehow, the dock seemed as narrow as a tightrope. I watched every step I took, trying my hardest to stay directly in the middle.

From the corner of my eye, I could see a patch of mangroves in the distance. I tried to ignore them, but it felt as if they were taunting me; it felt as if they were making fun of how easily they had trapped me. I could almost feel their vines around my ankle and their daunting presence hovering over me.

I continued walking, increasing my pace. The person I recognized still hadn't spotted me, and I wanted to reach him before he could run away. As I walked, people said hello when they reeled in their catches. The fish flailed and droplets of water just missed me.

As I neared the end of the dock, the person turned his head. A look of frustration crossed his face when he realized who I was.

"What are you doing here?" he asked. Even though he was angry, I could see the flicker of concern in his eyes. He knew the dock was a place that I never wanted to see again.

"Elliot, please let me talk to you."

I knew Jess had told me to leave him alone. I had done enough damage and it was time to let him be in control. Even so, I couldn't stand the thought of him deciding to leave me without telling him *exactly* how I felt.

"I thought I made it pretty clear that I didn't want to see you right now," he said, as he set his fishing pole down.

"I know, I know," I said, shaking my hands in front of me. "And everything you said was true." I paused and my voice began to quiver. "But what I said was true too."

His face softened, and he crossed his arms.

"When you said you were done fighting for us, I finally realized that I couldn't keep relying on you to put up with me. You were right. I treated you like you meant nothing to me." I put my hands on my face. "I don't know *why* I did that, but you really mean *everything* to me."

I choked out a sob and stepped closer to him. "I used to know exactly where my life was going. *Not anymore.* Everything changed in a matter of minutes. For all I know, I could still be scared to swim in five years. There were only a few things in my life that I thought would stay the same. Then, I ruined one of them."

"Emmi-"

"Elliot, I can't *imagine* my life without you!" I cried. "Even when I pushed you away, you pushed right back. Despite how much you were hurting, you helped me try and overcome my fear. I'm so, *so* sorry. I will never stop being sorry."

I took another step closer. "I know it didn't always seem like it. I know I should've said it a long time ago. But Elliot, I love you. I know for sure that I do. I love you so much."

I couldn't tell what he was thinking. His mouth was slightly open and he had an expression of shock on his face. It felt like hours passed, as he stared at me. I couldn't stand the thought of him saying he didn't feel the same way.

Then he closed his mouth and started to say, "Emmi, I-"

Before he could finish, he stepped on his fishing rod and it rolled, sending his legs back and his face forward. His head hit the dock so hard that he was knocked out, as his body fell into the water.

CHAPTER 39

AGAIN

I rushed over and peered into the murky bay. "Elliot!" Seconds passed and he didn't surface.

"Elliot!"

I looked towards the other end for help. Someone had started to power wash the side of a boat. With the whirring of the motor, no one could hear me. I turned back to the water. Elliot was still nowhere to be found.

I could hear my heart beating out of my chest and it got harder to breathe. I didn't have time to wait for an ambulance. He needed to be saved right now. *I* needed to save him right now.

"No, no, no, no, no," I gasped, as I kicked off my shoes. I put my feet right on the edge of the dock. I was hyperventilating. Everything in me revolted against what I had to do to save him.

I extended my arms in front of me and took deep breaths to calm myself down. My eyes welled with tears and my head pounded with reasons not to dive. But my heart pounded with the only reason that mattered.

I loved Elliot.

I closed my eyes, taking in my last sips of air. Then, with the most fear I'd ever experienced, I plunged into the water.

But my mind went blank.

I flailed my arms and legs, trying to remember how to swim. I couldn't tell which direction I was facing or how far I had sunk. My chest ached with fear when I recognized the inevitable.

No, no, no, no, no, no, no! I'm drowning! I'm drowning! How do I swim? Where is the surface? No, no, no, no! I can't breathe! No, no, no, no, no, no, no!

I kicked my leg and made contact with something.

It's Elliot!

Somehow, I found the courage to propel myself deeper into the water. The temperature dropped and the water darkened. My hands wrapped around his arms and I started pulling him up. He was completely limp, making it more difficult. Then I felt a pain shoot through my chest.

I can't breathe!

I swam as hard as I could, but I seemed to be getting slower and slower.

It's really going to happen. I'm going to drown this time.

My lungs begged for more oxygen. My mind went hazy. I slowed to a stop and looked down at Elliot. His eyes were closed and his hair billowed in the water.

Then I looked up and realized that I had made more progress than I thought. A burst of hope shot through me, as I adjusted my grip on him. With newfound energy, I surged upward.

When I broke the surface, I gasped for air. I ignored my fatigue and pulled his head above the water. He was still unconscious and I couldn't tell if he was breathing.

"Help!" I screamed.

I swam towards the dock and reached for it. I could barely get my hand over the edge, let alone lift him up there.

"Help!" I screamed again, my voice raspy with panic.

The weight of Elliot seemed to grow heavier, as I helplessly treaded water. I could barely see or hear anything anymore. I had to get out of the water. I had no other choice.

I put my hands around his underarms and started to lift him. It was no use. I just pushed myself further underwater. I tried again and failed.

"No," I cried. "No, no, no."

My eyelids were heavy, as I tried to stay afloat. Every muscle in my body was giving up. My legs kicked slower and water rose from my neck to my chin. I closed my eyes and pushed him into the air with all of my strength. But I just couldn't do it.

I was about to quit when suddenly, the weight was lifted from my arms. I let go of him and he didn't fall into the water. Then I felt hands on my shoulders, pulling me onto the dock.

I stopped moving completely, as my back was pressed against wood. I didn't know if my eyes were open; I couldn't see either way. My faint ability to hear turned into deafness.

The next thing I knew, I woke up in the hospital.

Again.

CHAPTER 40

DÉJÀ VU

As soon as I opened my eyes, I experienced the worst déjà vu I'd ever had. I saw the white ceiling of my hospital room, felt the familiar cotton bed sheets, and heard the exact same sighs of relief when my family noticed that I was awake.

"Emmi!" I heard Mom say. I turned my head in her direction and saw that Dad and Liam were also there. They looked concerned but definitely not as much as last time.

"Hey," I mumbled.

"How are you?" Liam asked, as he scooted closer to my bed.

"Fine. Just a little tired. How'd I get here?"

"Liz and a few others on the dock heard you in the water," Dad began, "and they found you trying to lift Elliot."

I sat up in my bed as it all flooded back to me. "Where is he? Is he going to be okay?"

"He's not awake yet, but the doctor is optimistic that he'll have a full recovery. He has a concussion," Mom added.

I relaxed a little. After he was passed out underwater for so long, I was worried things would be a lot worse.

"Anyway," Dad continued, "the ambulance brought you to the hospital, while you were both unconscious. The doctors said you blacked out due to an anxiety attack, which makes sense because you were in the water."

"How long have I been here?"

"About an hour. We moved the party to the beach, but we didn't tell them why. We didn't want to worry anyone."

I nodded. Then Dad asked, "Why exactly were you in the bay?"

"Well," I said slowly, "when we went to the marina to get bait, I saw Elliot fishing. So... I tried to talk to him."

I debated whether to continue, then I said, "I told him that I loved him."

My parents' eyebrows went up at the same time. Despite the situation I was in, the biggest smile spread across Mom's face.

"Really?" she said excitedly.

"Hold on," I interrupted. "Before he could say anything back, he stepped on his fishing rod, hit his head on the dock, and fell into the bay. No one could hear me yelling for help, so I had to save him myself."

I shook my head. "I almost drowned again, but I swam."

My family was filled with pure joy. Without saying anything, they all reached in and hugged me.

Just then, the door handle clicked. The four of us turned to see Liz peeking her head inside.

"Liz," I said, as I pushed my covers away and stood up. She ran to me and we embraced. I was never happier to call her my best friend.

"I'm so glad you're okay," she said when she pulled away and looked at me.

"Thank you so much."

"Oh," she said as she waved her hand. "I didn't do much. Do you really think I could lift Elliot?"

"No, Liz. Thank you for *everything*," I repeated. She smiled at me for a moment before hugging me again.

"I'd do it all over for you."

"Emiline?" came another voice from the door. It was a nurse.

"Yes?"

"You are cleared to go. Just make sure you sign out at the front desk."

"Okay, thank you," Dad said. When she left, I turned back to Liz.

"Have you seen Elliot?"

She hesitated, but replied, "No. He's not taking visitors right now."

"Okay. I'll stay here until he wakes up."

She sighed. "I knew you were going to say that. You shouldn't. You've done enough for him tonight."

"But-"

"Let's wait until tomorrow. You deserve to go home and get some rest."

I wanted to argue further, but I knew Liz wasn't going to budge. I looked at my family, but they agreed with her. So, I reluctantly left the hospital wing.

"Emiline Ganson is checking out," Dad said when we got to the front desk. When he started to complete the form, I noticed Liz wasn't next to me anymore. I looked around and spotted her standing far away, talking seriously to Mom, who nodded sadly. Then Liz walked back over to me.

"What was that about?"

"I'm driving you," she replied, as she took my arm.

"Okay? I'll see you at home," I said to my parents, while she dragged me out the door.

When we left the hospital, it was a dark and chilly night.

"Why did you want to take me home?" I asked when we got near the car. She didn't answer.

"Liz?" I repeated when I opened the passenger seat door. She still didn't answer as I sat down. "What are you-"

I looked where Liz was supposed to be sitting, but it wasn't her. She had gotten in the back. I thought my eyes were playing tricks on me when I saw who was sitting next to me. Her face was filled with nervousness, shame, and pain. My mouth hung open as I stared at her.

"Hi, Emmi."

"Nelly?"

CHAPTER 41

IT'S ALL MY FAULT

"**N**elly, what are you doing here?" I asked in total shock.

"Liz told me that you and Elliot were in the hospital. I wanted to make sure that you two were okay…"

I looked at her in disgust. "Why are you just *now* deciding to care?"

"Emmi, I-"

"A week ago or even yesterday," I interrupted, as I threw my hands up, "I would've been so happy to see you. It wouldn't have mattered that you abandoned me during the hardest time of my life. Nelly, I gave you *so* many chances to talk to me. But coming to the party was your last one. Choosing to visit me when I almost drowned *doesn't* make up for anything. You didn't even get out of the car!"

"I do care, Emmi."

"No, you don't!"

"I care so much that I couldn't bring myself to be around you."

"That doesn't make any *sense!*"

"It's all my fault…"

"What's all your fault?"

"The crash!"

Both of us went completely silent. Nelly put her face in her hands and Liz let out an upset sigh.

"Wh…" I shook my head. "What are you talking about?"

She sat quietly for a long time. She looked down, then up, then all around. Her mouth opened and closed like she was struggling to speak.

"Nelly?" I asked a little louder.

"It's all," she paused in frustration, "my fault."

It seemed like she wasn't quite looking at me, but rather into the past. It felt like she was peering angrily into a bad memory.

"You have to tell her," Liz said with gentle reassurance.

Nelly broke from her trance-like stare. She closed her eyes and took one more deep breath before she started to explain.

"When my mom woke me up for Sunday morning brunch the day of the accident, I was nervous and angry and confused all at the same time. I had so many excuses why I shouldn't go, but none of them worked. I could tell my family knew something was going on, but I just couldn't explain what had happened the night before. So, I stomped out the front door like a baby and didn't speak to anyone during the whole car ride. Do you remember how your family was the last to arrive?"

I nodded. Of course. I remembered every painful detail of that weekend.

"Well, my family was the first one there. We were actually a little early, despite my protesting. While we were waiting, Tommy and Jack were testing my patience, so I took a walk down the dock."

Then, her words started to sound as if it took all of her strength to speak them. "When I decided it was probably time to head back, I noticed a man sleeping on a wooden bench. Even though his phone was ringing, he wasn't moving at all, so I thought maybe something was wrong with him. I rushed over and nudged his shoulder a few times. Turned out, he was just in a deep sleep. He woke up saying things like *don't go* and *we can work it out* and some other name." She paused and swallowed. "That should've been a sign…"

"Of what?" I asked in disbelief.

"After coming to his senses, he told me he was just exhausted from getting no sleep the night before. I joked that I was exhausted with my friends. We both finished the walk back to the boat and said goodbye. He boarded the ship and I didn't give him another thought. I rejoined my family just as Liz arrived." She stopped talking and started to cry.

"I'm so stupid," she huffed.

"Nelly, what?" I demanded.

She took a few more deep breaths and continued. "He was wearing a white uniform with a hat and a name tag on his shirt. I was so wrapped up in my own drama that I didn't even question why he was dressed that way."

She wiped her eyes and finally gave me a desperate, sorrowful stare. "Then the crash happened. After you were rescued, we all went to the hospital and waited. It wasn't long after you had been settled in that I saw that man's face again."

My eyes grew wide with pleading, as I wished she would not say what I feared was coming.

"The man's picture was in Captain Benny's folder."

My mouth opened in shock. Out of every possible thing that could've happened, that was not what I had expected. At first, I was brimming with anger. She was right. She could've prevented so much pain.

"I don't know what to say," I muttered.

"I'm so sorry,"

"This is…" I stuttered, as I searched for words.

"I know, I know," she interrupted. Then she grabbed my hand and started to speak frantically. "I'm so *sorry*. I-I'm angry at myself every single day for not realizing what was going on around me."

"Why didn't you tell me what happened?"

"I guess I thought that if you knew, you would hate me. And even though you were mad at me for ignoring you, I didn't think it would be anything compared to your anger if you knew what really happened."

Then, all of my hatred melted away. I couldn't blame her. I couldn't blame anyone anymore. Although she could've stopped Captain Benny from getting on that boat, I didn't care. She was my best friend and I was just ready to have her back.

"I'll just go," she whispered sadly. "You don't have to tell me what you're thinking."

"Nelly, you were in the wrong place at the wrong time," I said as I grabbed her arm. "There were so many things that could've kept me from nearly drowning that day. Angelina and Captain Benny could've stayed together. Captain Tracey could've left for vacation a week later. We could've forgiven each other when we argued. I could've convinced my mom to let me stay in bed. Liz's mom didn't have to ask about the party. I didn't have to storm to the deck of the boat. Anyway, how were you supposed to know what was going to happen?"

I paused, as tears blurred my vision again. "I just want my best friend back." She looked at me for a few seconds before she spoke.

"And I want mine back too."

We wrapped our arms around each other and swayed back and forth, crying and laughing all at once. Then Liz joined in.

"We're back!" she said playfully.

In those minutes, I completely forgot about everything that was going on. I didn't care about anything except these two people with whom I'd spent my whole life laughing.

Finally, things felt a little more normal.

CHAPTER 42

THE WAVES KEEP CRASHING

While driving back to my house, I was overwhelmed with relief. I found myself looking at Liz and Nelly's smiles and feeling grateful. It was as if all of that worrying whether our friendship was over had just made us stronger.

When we arrived, we walked down to the beach. It was weird to think that even though so much had happened to me in those last few hours, the party had continued. Everyone was still celebrating their new beginnings. Barely anyone noticed that we were ever gone.

We spotted the classmate who had asked for more bait. He appeared to have completely forgotten about fishing, while he played frisbee with four others. I was a little frustrated that his want for bait contributed to Elliot and me ending up in the hospital, when it hadn't even been that important to him. But, in the end, maybe going to the marina was for the best.

Liz, Nelly and I took off our shoes and walked down to the shore. I could feel their concerned glances, as we got closer and closer to the tide.

I took a step forward as Liz and Nelly steadied my arms at the same time. I looked at each of them and smiled. I reached for their hands in unity and willed them to step forward with me. A wave came close but just missed us. We took one more step into the wet sand.

Then the next wave came and it rushed over our feet with force. The cold water shot through me and awakened all of my senses. I closed my eyes, listened to the rumble of the ocean and felt the white foam lightly popping on my ankles.

I didn't feel scared. I felt calm.

When the wave receded, I opened my eyes. Liz started to jump up and down, squealing with excitement. I laughed when she ran down the beach with Nelly following her. They yelled cries of victory, while they splashed and pushed each other.

Standing there in the night was the best moment of my life... the life that I still had. I knew nothing would ever go back to the way it was. Things were never going to be the same again, and that had to be okay. But I also knew deep down in my heart that I would swim again, despite how long it might take.

Ever since the accident, I felt like I'd been caught in a current that tossed me onto a rocky shore. Each time I got close to standing up, another wave pushed me down.

After all I'd gone through, I learned that there is no way to stop bad things from happening. No matter how hard we try, the tide will shove us back to the jagged shore.

But, I also learned that there will always be moments filled with happiness, laughter and love. The tide will be low and we will float with contentment.

Our lives are filled with the waves that keep crashing. We just have to be strong enough to stand up through it all.

EPILOGUE

NINE MONTHS LATER

My stomach lurched with every curve on the winding road. I couldn't quite pinpoint why. Was it because I was scared? Excited? Nervous? Overwhelmingly happy? Regretful? Was it because I was feeling all of those emotions at once? Most likely.

The hairband around my wrist snapped, finally giving in to all of the fidgeting I'd been doing. I looked at Jess when her eyes flitted over to me. But she didn't say a word.

It was the one-year anniversary of the accident, and we were visiting the dock where the boat left for its last dolphin watch.

When summer ended nine months earlier, I began college three hours away from home. I liked it there, even more than I had imagined. I was majoring in psychology, which was something I never would've considered if it weren't for meeting Jess.

Although I'd made other friends, Liz, Nelly, and I still remained close. We made trips to each others' colleges and always came home on the same weekends.

Because I was living somewhere else, Jess suggested that I hire a different, more convenient therapist, but I couldn't. Not only would a new one not understand everything I'd gone through, but I'd grown to love Jess like a sister and it would be impossible to replace her. So, we'd made adjustments and agreed to have two sessions a month. One in person and one over video chat.

She took a deep breath and turned to me. "Are you ready?" I looked her in the eyes and nodded. We got out and stopped in front of the car, linked our arms, and gazed at the dock.

Not long after the summer of the crash, Captiva Dolphin Cruises went out of business. Despite the company's constant explanation that it was a substitute captain, anyone who had heard my story decided not to take any chances. Even tourists stopped booking rides. Eventually, they weren't making enough money to pay Captain Tracey or any of the staff, and they had to close.

Staring at the dock, I could only picture what it used to look like. There were no longer signs stating the prices or praising the lovely views and food. The old-fashioned ticket booth had yellow tape wrapped around it, awaiting the day when it would be taken away. The dolphin statue was no longer there. The only trace that it ever existed was the orange and brown circle where its base used to be. In addition to all of this, the dock was empty. The boat that was only briefly used for dolphin watches was probably sailing somewhere else with some completely new purpose.

We walked away from the car. I stared straight ahead. I tried not to think about the benches to the right of me, especially the one where Nelly had found Mr. Benny.

We sat on the edge and dangled our feet over the ocean. Doing things like that didn't scare me anymore. Actually, a year later, I could confidently say that water didn't scare me at all. It just wasn't my life anymore. Yes, I swam on occasion, but it never felt like it used to.

Contrary to what I'd always pictured, there was never a defining moment when I conquered water. There was no rejoicing at the beach when I swam with all of the people I loved beside me. I didn't feel my fear slowly vanishing until it was gone. Then swimming just sort of happened.

Being there at the site of the accident, I pictured what I had been like the year before. I thought I had everything figured out. I was arrogant then. I was a completely different person now, and it was for the best.

I didn't fret over the little things anymore. Partly because I knew they weren't important enough to ruin relationships and partly because they didn't compare to everything else I'd experienced.

I also put others before myself so much more than I used to. I was everyone's priority for so long and in a way, I wanted to repay them.

And, more than ever, I cherished the people around me. I realized that I needed to understand how much they meant to me in the moment.

I touched my silver heart necklace when Jess put her arm around me. I looked at her and noticed she was crying. I didn't have to ask why. I felt the same way.

I rested my head on her shoulder and we sat in silence, small smiles on our faces and tears running down our cheeks.

We sat there until the sun set, turning the whole sky orange before disappearing below the waves.

ACKNOWLEDGEMENTS

When I began writing *The Waves Keep Crashing* at the age of thirteen, publishing, or even finishing the book didn't seem likely. I had never done anything like this before and had no idea where to begin. Now, after two whole years of writing, editing, rewriting, editing, and more rewriting, my book is published. But how in the world did a young teenager execute such a complicated task? The truth is, I wouldn't have been able to without so many amazing people to help me and most importantly, believe in me.

First of all, I would like to thank all of the teachers that helped me find my passion for writing. Suzy Daley, my fifth grade teacher, encouraged me to read more than anyone had ever before. Her lessons made me excited to write stories for the first time. She quickly became my friend and my go-to when talking about what I was reading.

Beth Fruchey and Jill Glass, my sixth and seventh grade teachers, kept me on track, reading and writing as much as possible.

Vicki Hermiller, my eighth grade teacher, helped me to see that publishing my book could be more than just a dream. As soon as I told her what I was working on, she was one of the most supportive people during this process. She was the first person to edit my rough draft and introduce me to the idea of publishing.

And Elisa Clevenger, my ninth grade teacher, helped more than she even realized. When I was becoming tired of looking at my same story every day, her picture wall of famous authors and students who had been published inspired me to keep going. In her class, I was reminded that when my book was done, all of the hard work would be worth it.

Second, I would like to thank my Grandma Verhoff, dad, and mom. When I was a little girl, my grandma and I would sit in her chair, pick from the overflowing basket of books, and she would read to me. At her house, I also wrote many little stories with construction paper, markers, and stickers for her and my grandpa to read. Now, she is reading another book that I wrote. (This one just might be a little better, though.) She was yet another person who constantly believed in me, no matter how impossible publishing a book seemed.

ACKNOWLEDGEMENTS

When I stuck my head out of our pool and told my dad for the first time that I was going to write a book, he didn't laugh or make any sarcastic remarks. He simply said something along the lines of, "Awesome. What's it going to be about?" because he simply knew I could do it. Throughout the writing process, he helped me research topics I wasn't familiar with (because researching is something he is very passionate about.) And whenever I felt unsure about my story while editing, he reminded me over and over that my feelings were normal and that I was a great writer. He encouraged me from start to finish and for that, I am very grateful.

I wrote the very first chapter of my book in my room on the night that I decided to start this journey. When I finished it, my mom sat on my bed and asked how it went. I remember saying, "That took longer than I thought it would." I had no *idea* how many more hours I would be putting into writing. From that night on, my mom was like a fully invested manager. She asked me about how writing and editing was going almost every day, even when I didn't feel like talking about it. She listened to me rant about writer's block, and even sparked ideas for two major plot points in the book. She read and edited *The Waves Keep Crashing* at work, even though I don't think that it was a great use of time. She even helped me to do something I do not normally do, use my voice, when asking stores on Captiva Island if they were interested in my book. Without everything my mom has done, I probably would've given up. Her constant faith in me is something I will always be thankful for.

Lastly, I would like to thank my editor and new friend, Beth Huffman. She agreed to help edit my story even though I was only fourteen years old. For almost an entire year, we worked on my book. She stayed up *way* too late editing my chapters and then calling me at least once a week to talk about them. She stuck with me throughout all of the additions and rewrites, even when I made it difficult. She was honest with me when she knew I could improve my writing and encouraged me to speak up when I didn't agree with her. She even guided my parents through the process of deciding where and how to publish my book. Most of the time, she was even more confident about my writing than I was. Her affirmations kept me going even when I didn't believe them. Without Beth, I truly do not know what would've come of *The Waves Keep Crashing*, and I hope that she realizes just how much I appreciate her.

ABOUT THE AUTHOR

When Ellie Keehn began this writing journey, she was only a seventh grader. That's when she said to her dad, "I have an idea for a story. I'm going to write a book."

This was the beginning of her quest to become a published author. Gifted with incredible writing skills and a creative imagination, Ellie penned *The Waves Keep Crashing* during her seventh and eighth grade years.

Throughout her freshman year of high school, she made meticulous additions to the story and nurtured the growth of the central characters. She was able to accomplish all this, while maintaining excellence as a conscientious student, a talented dancer, and a dedicated cross country athlete. Her other passions include reading, drawing and painting.

Ellie hopes to become a middle school language arts teacher and plans to continue writing. In fact, she already has an idea for her next book.